THE HANNIGAN SISTERS

THE HANNIGAN SISTERS: OAKWOOD BOOK TWO

First edition. December 22, 2019.

ISBN: 978-1393076872

Written by Tara C. Goddard.

Also by Tara C. Goddard

Oakwood
Dorian and Julia: Oakwood Book One[1]
The Hannigan Sisters: Oakwood Book Two[2]
Blue Falls[3]
The Rose Proposal[4]

Watch for more at Tara C. Goddard's site[5].

1. https://www.draft2digital.com/catalog/511173

2. https://www.draft2digital.com/catalog/511708

3. https://www.draft2digital.com/catalog/531831

4. https://www.draft2digital.com/catalog/564888

5. http://www.tcgoddard.com

OTHER TITLES BY TARA C. GODDARD

The Oakwood Series:
Dorian & Julia

THE HANNIGAN SISTERS

OAKWOOD BOOK 2

TARA C. GODDARD

© Goddard Collection 2019

THIS IS A WORK OF FICTION. Any resemblance to actual persons, or events is purely coincidental.

All rights reserved

No part of this book may be reproduced, or stored in a retrieval system, or transmitted in any form or by any means, electronic, mechanical, photocopying, recording, or otherwise, without express written permission of the author.

WWW.TCGODDARD.COM

CHAPTER ONE
Margo's Marriage

The cream-colored steamer her sister had bought her was starting to bubble, threatening to let out steam when Margo realized she had yet to put her dress on the hanger. The peach-colored dress, which she did not think she would like at first, had gotten wrinkled when her husband, Marius threw a stack of laundry on top of it in the bedroom. Marius was careless in that manner. Margo reasoned that he was a man and men didn't know anything about laundry. But today she was upset. This was the dress she wanted to wear. She and her friends Leona and Rumi agreed to wear light colors. The three women often wore dark colors.

As she put the dress on the hanger, she heard Marius walking up the stairs. They were more like stumbles rather than walks. Margo rolled her eyes, annoyed long before her husband was to come interfere with her preparations. *He's been drinking*, she thought to herself as she put on her panties and bra. Things were stale between the two of them for the past few months. Marius, a Software Developer, lost his job due to downsizing, and per Margo's observation, was not keen on getting a new one any time soon. She didn't mind supporting the family with her income as a bridal shop owner, but she hated that her husband was struggling to find motivation.

The last thing Margo wanted at the moment was for Marius to see her naked. In the past she would not have minded for the man she was married to for ten years to see her body. There was a time when the sight of him would set her heart racing. Things were different now. They were different. Even their moments of levity seemed to come with underlying jabs at one another. It was not all Marius' fault, that she could admit. Margo was beautiful. It was normal for her to be approached by other men, even in her husband's presence. And while she enjoyed flirting with others, she was aware of how it made Marius feel, to have to constantly fight for his wife's attention.

The stench of alcohol on his breath reached Margo's nose long before Marius completed his drawn out walk up the stairs. Margo worried about leaving the girls with him. Their two daughters, Emily and Charlotte, or the Bronte sisters as Margo liked to call them in jest, could not stay by themselves. She needed for Marius to keep an eye on them. The girls were sneaky and had a habit of causing trouble. Margo feared that in his state, Marius would not survive a night with the two of them on his own.

"Margo...Margo," he said as he leaned against the wall.

"Marius, what is it, don't you see I'm trying to get ready?" she responded.

"You're...you're so beautiful, it's scary," he said. Margo sighed.

"Thanks honey," she said as she continued to steam the dress.

Margo glanced across the bedroom at the clock on the nightstand. It was almost seven and she had to leave the house. She knew what Marius was up to. The man rarely deviated from his script. He'd come up and tell her how beautiful she was. She'd oblige him and say something nice in return. Then he'd complain about something, this time it was the fact that she was going to leave the house and leave him with the crazy girls as he liked to call them. Then naturally he'd make a play for her clothes. I suppose it's better that I didn't put the dress on yet, she thought as she steamed the dress.

"Honey, you can't leave me with the crazy girls," he said, hardly standing against the wall.

"Marius, you are their father. Figure it out," she replied, not looking at him.

"That's not fair Margo. I'm a little tipsy and I just don't think it makes sense that you are leaving me here with them," he said. He was now approaching her.

"Marius, I never ask you for anything. I don't get to see my friends often. So, I'm going to go out, and you are going to watch your children like a responsible adult instead of drinking all night," she said in a curt tone, flicking her brunette hair behind her as she finally turned to look at him.

"God, you're beautiful," he said.

"If you think I'm going to have sex with you right now, you must be out of your damn mind," she said. Marius stopped in his tracks, aghast at the suggestion that he was merely looking to have sex with his wife.

"Margo...that's not...why can't I pay my wife a damn compliment without being attacked?" he asked.

Margo finished with the steamer and quickly put the dress on. Marius stopped in his movement towards her. He seemed to be at a loss of words. Margo chuckled as she thought about the fact that this was a familiar dance between them. Yet there was a sense of loss that suddenly fell upon her. In the past, Marius would have insisted. He would have used sweet words in an attempt to convince her that what he offered was much more interesting than whatever she was going to find in a night out with her friends. She could always see the attempt at manipulation coming, yet she found it endearing that he was so eager to spend time with her. Now, any attempt of that sort smelled of desperation. He was a desperate man. And she did not know how to help him. Nor did she want to help him.

"Margo...I feel like..."

"When was the last time you applied for a job Marius?" she asked. She was putting on her deep red lipstick in front of the mirror in the master bedroom.

"I... why are you deflecting so damn much?" he asked.

"Marius, you go get a job and then we can talk about your feelings. Until then, your feelings don't matter, honey," she said in a sweet condescending manner.

"I really cannot stand you sometimes," he said.

A set of footsteps could be heard coming up the stairs. It was the girls, giggling, with their dolls in hand. They barged into their parents' bedroom without knocking and strolled past their father who was now sitting down on the king-sized bed, looking at the ground in front of him. Margo showered the girls with kisses and tickled them for a few minutes. Then her phone started going off. It was her friend Leona who was downstairs to pick her up.

"Girls, daddy is not feeling great so I'm going to need you to be on your best behavior," Margo said in a stern voice.

"He's been drinking," Emily said, her squeaky voice sounding like a mouse telling on a cat to its master.

"A lot," Charlotte concurred.

"I have not," Marius said, in a poor attempt at defending himself. The girls ran out of the room.

"Marius, you really cannot be drinking so much in front of the girls," she said.

"I... have a great night honey, we are going to be fine. I'm going to make some coffee," he said.

"Listen, you don't have to wait up for me okay?" Margo said. She kissed him on the cheek and left the room.

Marius followed behind Margo like a lost puppy looking for love. Despite her issues with his unwillingness to get a job, Margo loved him still. He still made her laugh. All the things that made their marriage strong were still there, but now there was a crack showing up. Not only was he not bearing his share of the weight, but Margo was beginning to eye another. As she passed by the kitchen, she glanced over at the flyer on the refrigerator. It had been given to her by her sister Marisa. It was for the annual picnic being thrown by the hospital where Marisa was an administrator. She looked forward to going, especially without her husband.

The next day, as she was getting lunch ready for the girls before heading to the park, Margo had a strange feeling that Marius wanted to talk to her. He had been nursing his cup of coffee in the living room, pretending to be watching the Sailor Moon episode the girls were watching. His eyes periodically glanced back to the kitchen.

The kitchen was open-ended, giving full view of the living room. Margo insisted on knocking the wall down when they bought the house so that she'd be able to see the Brontës if she was in the kitchen cooking. It was one of the many things the two of them were able to agree on in the early phase of their marriage.

Now, Margo was regretting her insistence on having that wall removed. She could feel her husband's burning eyes fixated on her. Margo returned home late the night before, being careful not to wake the girls. Marius was up, playing a video game through Steam, cursing at some thirteen-year-old a world away. Margo barely said a word to him when she came in, clearly intoxicated. He had sobered up by that time. He knew better than to badger her about being drunk. That was the beauty of the new power dynamic developing between the two of them.

Marius got up and walked into the kitchen proper, coffee cup in hand. That coffee must be cold by now, she thought as she cut the crusts off the sandwiches she was making for the girls. Marius came to her side of the kitchen island and grabbed a piece of salami and put it in his mouth.

"Whatever it is, please spit it out," she said, impatient to find out why he was leering in her personal space.

"You know you're not very nice to me," he said, "I'm your husband. You should speak to me in a gentler tone," he said. He playfully grabbed her by the hips.

"Marius, I have to finish this. I need to meet up with my sister at the park. They already started," she said.

"I did tell you I could make the lunches. I'm perfectly capable of making lunch for my children," Marius said. She scoffed.

"I know dear husband. It just makes me happy to do this for them," she said. They both knew she was being sarcastic, but neither was willing to fight about it. "Grace is going to be here at 12 to watch them so you can do whatever it is that you spend your day doing," she said as she cut the sandwich in half.

In the past this would have been the sort of day they would spend together as a family. Marius would have planned an event for them. Or they would have packed the car and headed to the park together. Those days seem to be distant now. It bothered Margo that her family life was falling apart. She was questioning being married to Marius.

As she pulled into the parking lot of the park, she noticed him from a distance. She hadn't seen him in a while. He used to come by the bridal shop just to chat with her. But in the past few years, he showed up less and less. He even stopped sending her Christmas cards. His light-colored brown hair was shorter now compared to the last time she and he sucked face with one another. Her heart was racing as she watched him and his best friend Dorian standing under the tent talking.

Nearby, was her sister Marisa, chatting with her best friend Julia. Margo liked Julia, though she found her to be a bit of a threat. Margo resented the fact that her little sister's best friend drew the admiring glances of men wherever she was. Julia, a blonde curly haired nurse, was the type of person who didn't hold back. She didn't cower in the face of a challenge. It was annoying when they were all teenagers, but Margo found it endearing as they became adults.

"So, you decided to skip the activities part of today?" Marisa asked as Margo approached her and Julia.

"Oh God, I don't do activities. Plus, after last night, it was a little hard getting up today," Margo said, "Hi Julia, you look great as usual," she added and kissed her on the cheek.

"Hi Margo...where's that dashing husband of yours?" Julia responded. Marisa scoffed.

"This is a strictly no husband day," Margo responded. The women laughed.

"I understand...I'm going to go bother Dorian for a little, I'll see you guys in a few," Julia said. She wrapped her arms around Marisa and attempted to pick her up.

"I'm afraid my sister has added a few extra pounds this month," Margo said and laughed.

"Margo! What the hell is your problem?" Marisa responded. Julia kissed Marisa on the forehead.

"You leave my Marisa alone Margo," Julia said playfully and left.

"I'm sorry, we can't joke about that? You said it yourself," Margo said as she grabbed her sister's hands.

"Just because I said it doesn't mean that I mean for everyone else to be discussing it. I'm sorry I'm not a waif like you Margo,"

"I'm sorry. I really am. I didn't know it was such a big deal for you," Margo said.

Harry, who had been eyeing the sisters for a few minutes, unbeknownst to them, walked across the tent, giving his friend Dorian and Julia breathing space. Marisa pulled on Margo's arm when she noticed Harry walking over. Marisa knew part of the reason Margo was not keen on her husband coming to the picnic was because she wanted an opportunity to speak with Harry without Marius hanging onto her body every minute. Margo and Harry's history together was an intense one. Having known each other since they were teens, Harry was very much head over heels in love with Margo. She used that fact to her advantage in every way possible. And Harry, even when he knew about her dalliances with others, looked the other way. It was during college, when he blossomed and became the handsome assertive person he was now, that Margo finally saw him as a good catch. However, by that time, he was involved with someone else. Theirs was a continuous case of missed moments, always coming close but never quite reaching.

"Well, aren't you just breathtaking," Margo said as he reached them. He kissed her on the cheek, and she hugged him tightly. Then he kissed Marisa on the cheek.

"Hey Harry," Marisa said, a wide smile on her face.

"Margo, we missed you earlier," Harry said.

"Margo doesn't do activities, she is too precious," Marisa responded. Margo smacked her sister on the arm, "well it's true," Marisa added.

"Yes, it is true, I'm not very athletic, you know that," Margo said.

"You sell yourself too short," Harry said. Margo chuckled.

"You're too kind Harry," Margo said. Then she gently kicked her sister.

"I'm going to get something to drink. I'll be back in a few," Marisa said. Harry smiled, aware of the machinations between the two sisters.

Harry and Margo walked over to a corner of the tent with few people crowding the space. Harry, with his well aligned pearly white teeth, grinned like a little boy seeing a girl naked for the first time. His gaze was fixed on Margo, to the point where she felt as though he might have been imagining her nude. It was a thought she did not mind. In fact, she'd love for him to imagine her naked. She liked the idea that even after having two children, a man outside of her husband found her attractive.

"Are you going to say something, or should we continue staring at each other?" she said. He chuckled.

"I'm perfectly fine with that," he said. She grabbed his right hand. She ran her finger across his palm.

"I'd rather we talk. The way you're looking at me is dangerous," she said.

"There's nothing wrong with a little danger," Harry said.

"Oh my God Harry, that's not good. You know I'm married right?" she responded.

"I might have heard a few whispers about that," he said.

"Whispers? Maybe you should stop talking," she said.

"So, I'm just going to stare into your eyes until your sister interrupts us," Harry said. Margo smiled.

A few minutes later, Marisa returned with a bottle of water in hand. She stood by as her sister and Harry stared at each other. Marisa was about to turn away when her sister tapped her on the shoulder.

"I have to run to the bathroom," Margo said, "will you keep this dream of a guy busy?" Margo said. Marisa rolled her eyes.

"Your sister is still a little crazy," Harry said as they watched Margo walk away.

"Yes, she is. I see you're still smitten," Marisa said. Harry chuckled. "My sister is truly beautiful, so I don't blame you," she added.

"Is she happy?" Harry asked.

It was a question Marisa had not had to answer in a long time. Though the two sisters were extremely close, they did not talk much about Margo's marriage. Marisa was never a Marius fan. She had done her best over the years to advise her sister to leave her husband due to his erratic performance as a husband and father. Yet Margo insisted that Marius was a good man and she did not envision ever leaving him because of his few flaws. That's marriage and you wouldn't understand, Margo would respond whenever Marisa asked her about why she dealt with Marius' less than stellar behavior as a husband.

"Honestly, I don't think she has been happy for a long time," Marisa said, knowing well that her sister would not be happy with her divulging information about her marriage to a man she clearly still had feelings for.

"Well, it's hard to reconsider when there are children involved," Harry said, the two of them barely looking at one another.

Marisa shrugged her shoulders. She thought about her own motives for saying what she said about her sister's marriage. To those who knew her well, but her sister, it was evident that Marisa was enamored with Harry. She did well to hide her desire for him in consideration for her sister's insatiable desire to possess men who are attracted to her. Marisa played that role for a long time and well. It was a role she learned to play from a young age. She had been attracted to her friend Dorian at a young age but dismissed her own feelings once she noticed how madly in love with him her best friend Julia was.

"I think she still loves you. So, take your shot. You will never get a better chance," Marisa said.

"It's that bad?" Harry asked.

"Does it really matter?" Marisa responded.

"I suppose it doesn't," he replied.

Harry and Marisa watched as Julia, looked intensely at Dorian as he spoke. The two of them laughed as they contemplated how two of their longtime friends seemed to have an awkwardness around one another. Marisa, being a good friend, knew exactly what Julia was going through. She knew what it was like to want to make something work with someone but always feeling as though things will never work out.

"I really hate what she's going through right now," Marisa said.

"Who?" Harry asked.

"Julia,"

"Can I tell you a secret?" Harry asked. They turned to face each other.

"Sure. I'm very good at keeping secrets," Marisa said. She took a sip of water.

"He is very much in love with her," Harry said, "Dorian is not a great communicator," he added.

"Unlike you," Marisa said.

"I'm not sure if that was a compliment or an underhanded shot," he said. Marisa laughed.

"No, I really mean it...If he still loves her, why doesn't he tell her?" Marisa said.

"Well, there is the ever-combatant Dr. Rooles who has her eyes and heart set for him. And they also have a past together,"

"It can't compare," Marisa said. Then she wondered if she had said too much. She did not think that Harry truly knew what happened between Julia and Dorian. And she did not want to end up saying something that would reveal information she had sworn to keep to herself.

"Hmm," he said.

"So, how's business treating you?" Marisa said in an obvious attempt to change the topic of conversation.

Just then, Harry noticed Margo walking back towards them. He smiled. Marisa watched him as his intense gaze returned. His eyes were meant for her sister, and she knew there was little she could do about it. She had been in her sister's shadow since they were kids. Margo was the oldest and the rebel of the family. But she was also perceived as the more beautiful with an outgoing personality who didn't ask for permission or forgiveness. She went for what she wanted, even if it meant hurting someone else.

Marisa tried to leave once Margo reached them, but Margo grabbed hold of her and gave her a sideways hug. It was the kind of hug you'd give someone you were friendly with but did not necessarily like. Margo winked at Marisa. Marisa was confused. She'd have expected Margo to hint that she makes her exit so that she could speak with Harry a little longer.

"That bathroom was a lot farther than I remembered," Margo said. She too was doing her share of staring now.

"You should have asked for a guide,' Harry said. Margo laughed.

"That's funny, I'm sure you would have volunteered Harry," Margo said.

"Oh, he definitely would have volunteered," Marisa said.

"It would be pathetic of me to pretend I wouldn't take pleasure out of that," Harry said.

"Jesus," Marisa said.

"Don't mind my sister Harry. She was born grumpy," Margo said.

A few minutes later, Julia, her curly blonde hair in a bun, returned to the three of them to let them know everyone was going to meet up at a bar a little later. They were all expected to be present. Margo felt uneasy about the invitation. As much as she wanted to spend more time talking with Harry, she did have a husband and a family at home. Marius would not have minded her staying out drinking, she thought. But the truth was that he wouldn't have dared to vocalize his objection to her being out drinking. He had been doing his fair share of disappearing and going out drinking with his friends. And she never gave him a hard time about it.

Margo wanted to reconnect with Harry, but she did not want to jeopardize her marriage. At least not yet. She thought about the fact that her girls would not eat dinner or brush their teeth without her insistence. Margo was good at getting her girls to cooperate. They simply trampled over Marius. On the rare occasion that they weren't ignoring their father's requests, they still negotiated whatever task they were asked to complete.

"I really can't," Margo finally said as her sister was getting ready to leave.

"Why not?" Marisa asked.

"I have to get home. You know the Brontës are just going to eat him up. And... I don't know, I don't want to end up doing something," Margo said.

"For God's sake Margo, you've been talking about how great it is to see Harry again. You've got to take every opportunity you have to be around him. Don't be stupid," Marisa protested.

"Marisa, I'm married. You do remember, that right?"

"You only remind me once an hour," Marisa said, her tone spiking up more than usual.

"I'm sorry but am I irritating you?"

"Margo, you and I have this conversation over and over. You know Marius is no good. You gave it a good run. Are you really going to continue sacrificing your happiness and desire just to stay with him?" Marisa said.

Harry rejoined the two sisters after chatting with some of the other attendees. While Margo felt she would regret not going to the bar with everyone, she also knew that this was not the only opportunity she would get to see Harry. She imagined it made sense for her to go home and give Marius the illusion that she was still committed to their marriage, despite her disdain. And when she hugged Harry while saying goodbye, she held on a little longer than usual, breathing in his essence.

"You really can't come?" Harry asked in one last attempt to lull her into spending time with him.

"Married life, sorry." she responded. Then she kissed her sister on the cheek, "don't do anything stupid." she said to Marisa.

"Only one of us is making a stupid decision here," Marisa said, "C'mon Harry, let's go," she added. Margo watched as her sister and Harry left.

CHAPTER TWO
Harry's Wooing

Harry pulled up in front of the bridal shop in his rented Mercedes with a bouquet of gardenias on the seat next to him. He was sharply dressed and well accessorized. When he removed his sunglasses, he opened the top mirror in the car to make sure he didn't have crumbs on his face, right before he popped a breath freshener in his mouth. He knew what he was about to embark on was a challenge. But he viewed it with the same strategic approach he'd taken with his business ventures.

An hour earlier, he had walked into a floral shop down the street from his hotel looking for flowers to bring to Margo at work. The woman behind the counter, after marveling about how well-dressed he was, suggested that he get gardenias if he wanted to seduce the woman he was interested in. Harry imagined it would be good to bring Margo some roses. That was a classic winner as far as flowers were concerned. Yet after some persuasion, he was convinced that the smell of the gardenias would work perfectly in his attempt to win Margo away from her husband.

The chime from the front door went off as soon as Harry opened the doors. A slender young woman with a look on her face that suggested she'd rather be anywhere but work right at that moment, popped her head up to see who had entered. Then she walked from behind the counter and over to Harry. He smiled at her, but she gave him no response. Then she noticed the flowers in his hand.

"I'm sorry, how can I help you? Did you have an appointment with one of the consultants?" the young woman asked, confused as to why a man was walking into a bridal shop with flowers.

"No, I..."

"Are you from the new flower shop on Langley? We already have floral shops that we work with, and there is a clear no solicitation sign on the door," she interrupted. Was there a sign? He wondered. He hadn't noticed a no solicitation sign.

"No, I'm not a florist. I'm here to see Margo," he said.

"With flowers?" she asked. Harry chuckled.

"Yes, with flowers, that's not so strange is it?" he asked.

"Nancy!" the young woman shouted behind her. A short petite woman came out with a measuring tape around her neck.

"What happened Ashley?" the woman said.

"This man...I'm sorry what was your name?"

"Harry," he replied.

"Harry here said he is here to see Margo...he brought flowers," Ashley said.

"Oh, is that so. And with flowers, that's an interesting choice," Nancy said. Another woman came out from the back as if they had been waiting offstage for their opportunity to inspect the new entrant.

"What is going on here?" the woman, a tall redhead with a stack of metallic bracelets on her left wrist asked.

"Oh Rosie, this is Harry. He is here to see Margo...he brought flowers," Nancy said.

"Yes, I have flowers," Harry said, amused by this train of women who seemed dumbfounded by the idea that he would show up to her work with flowers.

"Ballsy," Rosie said. Then she took out her phone and dialed. "Hey Margo, there is a Harry waiting down here for you. He brought flowers," Rosie added. Harry chuckled.

"You have nice teeth," Ashley said.

"Oh...thank you," Harry said.

Silence fell over the room as Harry stood by with the flowers in hand waiting for Margo to come down the stairs. The women, who seemed to have nothing else to do at the moment, stood in front of Harry, staring. The heat coming from their eyes as they judged him without using their words. He hadn't felt that uncomfortable since he was a sprouting eight grader being grilled about a stolen test.

A few minutes later, which couldn't have come any sooner, footsteps could be heard from the back end of the bridal shop. Margo, in a yellow dress that hugged her body, came out from the back. The women parted, as if by command, making way for her to come through.

"I don't pay you guys to stand around, do I?" Margo asked.

"Why did he bring flowers?" Rosie asked.

"Because he's a gentleman, now buzz off," Margo responded as she hugged Harry.

"Mhhhm" Rosie said.

"Harry, why don't you come into my office. The rest of you, please go find something to do," Margo said and started walking toward the back. Harry followed behind her.

Harry's gaze had not waned as he followed behind Margo up the stairs. And she walked in a manner carefully designed, to lure his attention. At the top of the stairs, she glanced back at him as she opened the office door. He smiled his charming smile and she opened the door. The office was large with samples of dresses on mannequins. On top of selling wedding dresses, Margo was also a designer and was working on a new set of wedding dresses. She walked straight to her desk and leaned against it.

"Gardenias, the lady told me they were great for seduction," he said. Margo laughed.

"Is that what you're playing at Harry? Are you going to seduce me?" she asked as he handed her the flowers. Harry chuckled.

"Is it working yet?" he answered. She shook her head.

Harry leaned against a gray chair nearby. He continued looking at her as she smelled the flowers. Then Margo opened a closet near the door of her office and took out a tall vase. She removed the flowers from the paper wrapping they came with and placed them in the vase. As she walked back to her desk, Harry reached out and pulled her by the waist. Margo giggled.

"What are you doing?" she asked.

"Bringing you closer to me," he replied.

"Harry,"

"Margo,"

"Harry, I really can't. You know I'm married,"

"So, it appears," he replied. She wriggled her way out of his grasp and placed the vase on the table.

"Would you like some coffee?" she asked as she walked over to a small white table by the window.

On top of the table was a silver coffee pot as well as three small coffee cups. She poured coffee into a cup, not waiting for him to give her an answer. Then she walked over to him, being careful to leave some distance between them as she handed him the coffee. Harry looked at the cup, then looked at her. Then he smiled.

"You'll have to go downstairs if you want some milk or sugar, I only drink coffee black," she said. He nodded.

"This is perfectly fine," he said. He took a sip of the coffee then he moved closer to her. "It's easy to forget how beautiful you are sometimes," he said. She sighed.

"Thank you, Harry," she said as her skin started to turn a little red. "How...how long are you...you're moving your business here right?" she added as he moved a little closer.

"Am I making you uncomfortable?" he asked as their faces became closer to one another.

"I've missed you Harry," she whispered.

Harry touched the soft skin of her cheek and she moved her face in his hand. They stared at one another. But when Harry leaned in to kiss her, Margo put her finger on his lips. She pulled her head back a little, and then gently pushed him back. Harry chuckled as Margo skipped on her way behind her desk.

"Harry you really have to stop," she said.

"Stop what? I'm merely trying to get in touch with an old friend. What's wrong with that?" he asked.

"Old friend? Ha-ha, we were more than that," she said.

"And we can be once more. If you'll stop fighting it," he said with a sly smile.

"God, you're such...I really do miss you Harry, but I'm married. And you have to understand, as much as I like you, I can't really..."

"Margo, I'm not asking you to marry me," he responded.

Harry hadn't thought about asking Margo to marry him, even when the two of them were together. Marriage was not the sort of thing that crossed his mind. Yet at this moment, he found himself wondering what he was asking her to do. He understood that she had put time and work into her marriage, yet he also understood that within Margo lied a carnal desire that Marius failed to keep up with.

He recalled the day he heard she was getting married. He was on a boat off the coast of Fiji. He had been invited by a wealth management client of his to join a group of other businesspeople on this trip. It was then that he received the call that Margo was getting married. When he returned to London, where he was living at the time, there was a wedding invitation waiting for him. Harry contemplated for a long time about what to do. He wanted to respect her decision to marry Marius, but he felt a sinking feeling in his gut about Margo marrying someone who did not match her enviable joie de vivre.

"Are you happy?" Harry finally asked to break the silence. Margo sighed.

"It ebbs and flows," she said. He sat down on the chair as he sipped the coffee.

"From what I hear, there have been more downs than ups," he said. She laughed.

"My sister needs to shut up about my marriage," she said. Harry smiled, revealing in that moment who the source of his information was.

"You deserve to be happy," he said, "I mean, you know that already. And I can tell,"

"Tell what?" she asked. She sat up a little, revealing her neckline to him. He gulped.

"I can tell you're a little restless," he said. She laughed.

"You know that they think we're up to no good up here," she said.

"Shouldn't we give them something to gossip about?" he asked. She shook her head.

"You know, Ashley is Marius' little cousin. So, when I leave here, I'm sure I'm going to have to have a conversation with my husband about why a tall striking man with a charming smile brought me flowers at work," Margo said.

Harry knew she was right. Though he may not have known Marius, he knew enough about relationships to know that it is never a good thing for a man to show up with flowers for a woman who was not his wife. Harry smiled as he thought about the evergreen country song that was this romantic dance happening between, he and Margo. He was confident enough to know that his presence awakened something in Margo. She was doing her best to fight off whatever she might have been feeling about him.

Harry got up from the chair and walked over to the little coffee table and poured a little more coffee into the cup. The phone on the desk started ringing and Margo motioned to him that she had to answer it. And as she talked on the phone, Harry carefully watched her, as if he was looking for an answer to a formidable puzzle. Whenever she had a little break during her conversation on the phone, she'd look up at him and smile.

While Margo talked with her client, Harry perused the photo albums on her desk. There were pictures of her family, her husband and two girls. As well as a picture of her and her sister Marisa. It was in looking at that picture that Harry decided the best thing he could do was to enlist Marisa in his attempt to reconnect with Margo. He knew that despite the fact that she appeared to be unhappy in her marriage, she was stubborn enough to think she could make it work. Marisa would know more about Margo's state of mind than Harry could deduce on his own. He sipped his coffee carefully as he watched her lips move as she commanded the conversation.

"I'm sorry about that, it was a call I was waiting for before you came," she said.

"No need to apologize," he said, "I really should get going and let you work," he added. She walked out from behind the desk. He put the coffee cup down.

"It's so good to see you Harry," she said as she hugged him.

"It's even better to see you Margo," he replied. He kissed her on the cheek.

"God Harry, timing has always been..."

"Margo, you know I don't care that you are married. You and I... there's always been that fire between us. There will always be that fire. And I know you have to be respectful of your marriage, but I don't need to be," he said. She was surprised by what he said.

"Harry, you're going to be trouble for me. I can't afford that right now," she said. There was a knock on the door. They released one another. "Come in," she said. Rosie entered.

"Sorry I hope I wasn't interrupting anything," Rosie said.

"No Rosie, what is it?" Margo answered.

"That woman from last week is here with her dress," Rosie said.

"I'll be going, nice to meet you Rosie. We'll talk Margo," Harry said as he left.

Driving through Oakwood was the type of mental exercise Harry enjoyed most when he lived in the town. Harry always wanted to drive the well-maintained streets of the northwest quadrant. And it was this affinity for the city of his youth and the sudden coalescence of all the people who meant something to him in this one space, that drove his decision to move his lucrative business to the town. He hadn't imagined that he would seek a connection with Margo again.

Time was an equalizer in their romance. While she did not appreciate him when the two of them were together, she grew to see what everyone else saw. That he was confident in himself and what he had to offer. He was the sort of man who avoided making irrational promises and delivered on what he promised.

As he drove through the town to go to the location on Rossart Avenue where he was to meet the property manager, Harry thought about his desire for Margo and how selfish it was of him to put her in a position that made her uncomfortable. Yet he was aware that part of what drove his success was a willingness to push the boundaries and make people see what they weren't sure was there to begin with. He knew that Margo's fire was dying in her marriage with Marius. And if he was good at one thing when it comes to loving someone, it was turning the light on, and keeping it burning.

The building, from the outside was in pristine condition. And as Harry pulled up in front of it, he wondered why the office space had been left empty for the past three months. A portly gentleman with fiery red hair and a blue denim jacket on stood in front of the space flicking through a small binder.

"Mr. Melville!" the red-haired man shouted as Harry exited the car, "It's me, Roger. We spoke on the phone,"

"Hi Roger, nice to finally meet," Harry said as they shook hands.

"We can head right in, I have the keys," Roger said. Harry wondered what they'd do if he didn't have the keys, but he didn't want to come across as rude by pointing out how obvious it was that Roger would have the keys to the office.

Harry walked through the office, behind Roger as the red-haired man spoke with running speed. The place was a basic space that would fit a couple of offices. Harry intended on having an office for himself, a conference room and a desk for a secretary. So, the place was more than adequate.

"There are a few other business owners who are really interested in this space, so you should probably make a decision soon," Roger said in an attempt to create a sense of scarcity.

"It's been on the market for three months and no one has taken it. I'm not an idiot Roger," Harry said. Roger chuckled.

"Mr. Melville, I don't mean anything...that's not what I meant,"

"It's okay Roger, you're just doing your job. I like the place. I will need to have an independent contractor come and check for mold and all that, is that going to be a problem?" Harry said. Roger shook his head.

"No problem Mr. Melville, no problem at all."

"And please stop calling me Mr. Melville. Harry will do,"

"Okay Harry sounds good. You just let me know when you want to have someone come look at the place," Roger said as he closed his binder and tossed the keys in his jacket pocket.

"I'll be in touch Roger" Harry said and returned to the car.

Harry took the scenic route on the outer edges of Oakwood, near the Ravenswood crossing line to get to his next destination. He hadn't planned on going there at first, but after the time spent in Margo's office, and the sort of energy he felt from being in her presence. Marisa and Margo were the best of friends, even though they often bickered. No one would know Margo better, he reasoned as he weaved in and out of lanes on his way to the Oakwood General Hospital.

Harry hopped out of the car when he parked in the parking lot. It was the lot intended for hospital employees, but he did not care. He did not own the car and his insurance that he paid a premium on would cover any fees associated with the vehicle being damaged or towed. And as he was walking towards the hospital entrance, he noticed Julia's car. She was seated behind the wheel, simply staring out. Something must be wrong, he thought as he approached her car. The Julia he knew, was full of life and energy. He knocked on the car window. Julia screamed as she was startled by the sudden knock on the door. Then she lowered her window.

"Christ Harry, are you trying to give me a heart attack?" Julia asked.

"What are you doing staring out into space like this?" Harry asked.

"Pfft...Harry, I just needed," she started but Harry did not hear her as he was walking around her car to the passenger's side.

"You really should clean your car out sometimes," he said as he moved her bag to the back seat.

"Oh, please come into my car and judge me," she said.

"Don't be dramatic Julia. What's going on?"

"It's nothing," she said.

"It's Dorian isn't it? What did he do?" Harry asked.

"I don't really feel like talking about it Harry. Is that okay?" she said. He nodded.

Having known Julia almost all his life, Harry knew that when she said she didn't want to talk about something that didn't really mean that she didn't want to talk about it. What it meant was that she did not want to talk about it with him. And he was okay with that. People in Julia's life, from time to time have gotten used to reading the subtle messages she sends out without being offended. Harry was one of the best at reading her. Yet he pitied her. Julia's relationship with his best friend Dorian had become a strained one, where each person circumvented the work necessary to fix the turmoil driving them apart.

"Why are you here?" Julia asked.

"To see you beautiful," he said. She chuckled.

"You're such an idiot," she said. He nodded.

"I'm not going to deny that,"

"But really..."

"I'm here to see Marisa. I want to see if she'd help me out with Margo. I can't quite figure out my angle. I know there is something there, her marriage notwithstanding,"

"Oh yeah, other people's marriage can be such a bummer," Julia said, and he pinched her.

"Hey, don't make fun of me," he said.

"So, if I understand this correctly, you are here to ask Marisa for help in wooing her sister?' Julia said.

"Wooing, oh what a fantastic word," he said.

"God, men are so clueless sometimes," Julia said.

"What?"

"Oh, I'd love to peel the blindfolds off, but it's really not my business. I've become really good at minding my own business," she said.

"I mean..."

"Get out of my car so I can finish wallowing," she said. Harry chuckled.

"You know, you and Dorian are so perfect for each other. You're a little crazy, and he can't ever say what is on his mind without pissing someone off," Harry said.

"That makes no sense Harry," she said as he opened the car door. Harry blew Julia a kiss and closed the door.

When he got off the elevator, the receptionist sitting behind the desk sat up and fixed her dress. Harry, oblivious to the effect he was having on the older woman behind the desk, walked up to the desk and signed the visitor's log without once making eye contact with her. The woman, whose name was Rebecca, looked up at him from her chair, waiting for him to say something. When he was done signing, he looked around the waiting room and then turned back to Rebecca.

"Hi, I'm here to see Marisa, I mean Ms. Hannigan," he said. Rebecca fixed her glasses.

"Ms. Hannigan just stepped out for a little bit, she has to do some trainings for the doctors," she said, "sexual harassment training," she added as she covered her mouth and whispered as if there was someone else in the office who didn't need to hear what they were talking about.

"Oh okay, I'll wait," he said.

"Okay," she said as she looked at the visitor's log for his name, "Mr. Melville," she added.

Harry plodded down on one of the brown leather couches, crossing and uncrossing his legs like a man unused to having to wait. He'd occasionally look at his watch, although he did not have anywhere to go. And on the occasion that he looked up toward the receptionist's desk, he caught Rebecca staring at him as if he was a statue from Rome. rather than let his boredom consume him, Harry got up and walked over to Rebecca. Again, the woman sat up, fixing her dress as if she had been wriggling around in it.

"How long have you worked for Marisa?" he asked. She cleared her throat.

"Five years now. Five. She really is a wonderful boss," Rebecca said. "I sent her a message that you were here, so it won't be long," she added.

"Thank you, Rebecca," he replied.

"How...how do you know Marisa?" she asked.

"Pfft...since we were probably in Elementary school. We grew up here in Oakwood," he answered as he grabbed a mint candy from the bowl in front of Rebecca.

"You can have more if you want. People always think you can only take one. And sometimes, I wish they'd take more than one," she said and chuckled. Harry smiled. "You have a beautiful smile Mr. Melville." she added.

"Thank you, Rebecca, that's kind of you.

"Harry! Hey, what are you doing here?" Marisa's voice came booming from behind Harry. When he turned, she had a bright smile on her face.

"Hey," he said and kissed her on the cheek, "I wanted to see your office, and also ask you for a favor," he added.

"Come into my office. Do you want some coffee? Rebecca can you get Harry some coffee?"

"Oh, no, I think I've had enough coffee for the day. Thank you, Rebecca," he said.

"My pleasure Mr. Melville," she said and winked at Marisa.

Marisa's office was much larger than her sisters. And as Harry entered, he chuckled. He remembered that the sisters competed against one another. He also recalled that it was their father who encouraged their sort of ruthless competition with one another. He walked around the office for a few minutes, looking in every direction, taking in the view from the window. Meanwhile, Marisa did her best to keep her composure, unwilling to talk first lest she say something to embarrass herself.

"This is a great office Marisa," he said, "how come you've never invited me here before?"

"Oh...Harry I didn't think you cared about my work...and... you also travel a lot, I'm sure you've seen much better offices around the world," she said. She pressed a button on her telephone set to route all calls to voicemail.

"Well I would have liked an invitation all the same. You and I used to be such good friends," he said.

"I'm sorry Harry, I didn't think it mattered to you. I'll remember that next time I get a kick ass office," she said. He laughed.

"I went to look at a space today for my office,"

"Did...did you like it?" she asked.

"Yeah, it's nice, and I think I'm going to steal Rebecca from you. She's a lovely woman and my clients would love being greeted by someone like her,"

"You can't take my Rebecca Harry, that's out of the question. And there's no one like her. She is the best receptionist I've ever had," Marisa said, "um...you said you needed my help with something?" she asked. Harry finally walked to the chair in front of her desk and sat down.

"So, here's the thing. I need your help with Margo," he said.

"Oh," she said disappointingly.

"I know she's married, and I know it means a lot to her. But like you said, things don't seem to be on the up for her and her husband. And I feel like there is a part of her that she's had to sacrifice for this marriage. Look, I know that she's feeling something for me at the moment, I can tell when she is around me. There is a sort of energy that comes through, and I want to recapture that," he said.

Marisa mused about what he said for a few minutes. Margo had been unhappy in her marriage. At least that was the message she sent her sister on numerous occasions. And Harry was right about Margo having to sacrifice a part of herself for the sake of her marriage. She had become a far more domesticated person than she ever was. She spent less and less time with her friends, though they meant the world to her.

"Okay, Harry, I'll help you in whatever way I can," Marisa said, accepting that she too was capable of making sacrifices, even if the man sitting in front of her did not recognize her act as a selfless one.

CHAPTER THREE
The Sisters In Love & Life

The bright morning sun enlivened Margo on Saturday mornings. She made it a ritual get out of bed before her husband and her children to sit in the lounge chair in the backyard, to let the sun bathe her skin before the demands of the day took over. It was going to be a day like all other Saturdays. Her husband would wake up from a night of hard drinking and then head out to go play flag football with his friends. The girls would have many questions about their aloof father's whereabouts and Margo would invent some story to tell them. She'd spend the rest of her day either cleaning or talking on the phone with one of her friends lamenting the fact that they no longer spent time together at brunch the way they used to in their twenties.

The thought of her mundane life made Margo laugh as the sun hit her skin in the backyard. The waking sounds of the animals nearby were more soothing than she remembered. The one thing, she decided, that made this Saturday different was that she could not stop thinking about Harry. The very idea of him made her hot and bothered. Though she pretended it was all the sun's doing. She smiled as she thought about the flowers, he brought to her at work and the way he looked at her. She had been married to Marius for ten years, and he did not look at her that way. She couldn't remember if her husband ever looked at her with that discerning look. It was a look that sexualized a woman without lurking. It was a look that recognized both her beauty and her essence, and capacity for love. It was the sort of look that communicated desire with the fire from one's own body. Marius didn't look at her like that. Marius saw her beauty. And in some ways, he was grateful that someone as beautiful as Margo agreed to marry him. But he did not look at her as if he needed to possess her. If Marius had an animalistic desire in him, Margo had never seen it. Despite his drinking and his joblessness, and his inability to get the girls to do what he wants, Margo believed Marius to be a good man. He was a loving husband, if not a great lover.

It didn't take long after she laid in the lounge chair for her to hear noises coming from inside the house. Margo sighed, she knew her moment of peace and tranquility was coming to an end. Charlotte came out of the house in her pajamas, and barefoot. She was rubbing her eyes as she walked to her mother. Without saying a word, Charlotte climbed her mother and lay on her body as if she was a long body pillow. The girl rested her head on her mother's chest, matching her breathing with hers. As much as she would have liked to protest this sudden invasion of personal space, Margo loved her girls and she loved these moments when her children took over her body without asking, as if they were owed this sort of access to their mother's physical space. She smiled as she ran her hand through Charlotte's hair.

"Mommy?" Charlotte said in a quiet voice.

"Yes darling?"

"I'm going to be hungry soon,"

"You're predicting your hunger?" Margo asked.

"Yes," Charlotte said, "but not right now. I like this. I want to stay like this forever," she added.

"Well...if we stayed like this forever, we would never get anything done, let alone eat food," Margo said.

"I miss you," Charlotte said, digging her face into her mother's breasts.

"I see you everyday sweetheart...careful, that hurts a little," Margo said.

"Just because you see someone doesn't mean you're spending time with them. You always leave us with daddy, or grandma," Charlotte said.

Margo could not fight against what her daughter was saying. Since she returned to work at the bridal shop, she was spending less time with the girls. And since Marius was out of work, she figured he could take care of them, something no one in the house thinks he is good at, himself included. Margo felt guilty that her daughter felt the way she felt, but she didn't want to have to sacrifice her business simply for the sake of playing with her children.

"How about once a week you come to the shop with me? After school. We can hangout and I can show you how we make women's dreams come true?" Margo said. Charlotte popped her head up.

"I'd love that," she said.

"Good, it's a deal then," Margo responded.

Margo and Charlotte lay on the lounge chair for another ten minutes before they heard noises coming out of the house. It appeared that Marius and little Emily were arguing with one another. Emily, the youngest child, was also the one who tested her father's resolve the most. She was in every way, a carbon copy of her mother, something Marius was keen on pointing out. Margo and Charlotte got up and went back into the house to see Emily running away from her father as he tried to put clothes on her.

"She won't get dressed!" Marius shouted. Standing by the couch in the living room, was Margo's sister Marisa.

"Marisa, when did you get here? Marius just leave her alone; she's not going anywhere this morning. If she wants to run around naked, let her," Margo said.

"I just came. I brought bagels. You make the coffee," Marisa said. Charlotte ran up to her aunt and hugged her.

"This is ridiculous, I have to get going to my game. You deal with her," Marius said, his face flushed red as his frustration grew. "She's just like you. It's so unbearable," he said as he walked back up the stairs to the bedrooms.

While Margo and Marisa headed into the kitchen, Charlotte took the clothes her father left on the floor and started dressing her sister. Emily did not think once to fight her sister on getting dressed. It was a special bond that they had.

It was unlike Marisa to pop up at her sister's house without calling first. And Margo made a mental note to ask her sister about it, though she refrained from doing so while the girls were around. She wanted to model good sisterly relationships in front of her girls as they will be attached to one another for their entire lives. As the coffee machine beeped to signal that it was ready, Marius ran downstairs, half staring at his watch and eyeing the coffee machine. He grabbed a portable cup and poured coffee in it, never thinking to ask the women in the kitchen if it was okay if he took some.

"I should be back around twelve," he said and kissed his wife on the cheek.

"Unless you go drinking afterwards," Margo said.

"Unless I go drinking afterwards," Marius repeated as he exited the kitchen to say bye to his daughters.

"You guys kiss each other on the cheek?" Marisa asked. Margo sighed as she poured coffee in two red mugs.

"That is the state of our marriage sis," Margo said and handed Marisa a mug.

"That's not healthy. There's like no sensual energy between you two, everything is…"

"A transaction," Margo said.

The sisters joined together to make a breakfast of waffles and strawberries for Charlotte and Emily. The kitchen, which had been quiet but for the brewing sound of the coffee machine, was suddenly full of people as the girls sat at the kitchen table drawing and laughing. While Margo and Marisa prepared their breakfast. And when they were done cooking, they put plates in front of the girls and exited the kitchen.

Of the few things that Margo was confident about, it was in Charlotte's ability to look out for her sister. She sensed even when Charlotte was much smaller, that she would be the caring one while Emily would be the rabble rouser. Sometimes, Margo imagined that she had projected these personalities onto her children. She and Marisa were very much like Charlotte and Emily. The only difference was that she was the rabble rouser and Marisa was the caring one.

"Let's go to the backyard, the sun is really beautiful this morning," Margo said, coffee mug in hand. Marisa followed after her.

They each pulled a lounge chair and lay on it. Unlike Margo, Marisa did not enjoy the morning sun quite as much. Her sister joked that she was paler than anyone she had ever seen, while Margo was sun kissed, an achievement that requires dedicated practice and an affinity for leisure.

"There is no point in staying with him Margo," Marisa said, finally revealing what had been on her mind.

"I was wondering how long it was going to take before you said that," Margo said. She took a sip of her coffee and looked into the distant horizon.

"Margo, you know I don't say things lightly. What you guys are doing is not healthy. You are not very nice to him, and he's kind of just falling apart and he can't even admit it,"

"Oh, so it's my fault?" Margo protested. She turned to look at her sister.

"Margo, you know that's not what I'm saying. But you two haven't been in love for a long time. What's the point of this charade? Neither of you are happy," Marisa said.

"He just needs to find a job,"

"Margo, you know it's not about the job. You're not suffering for money. You can be the breadwinner. There is something else there. There is something missing. When I see other married people, there is a light in their eyes when they look at each other. There is a sense of love. You two look like you're housemates raising two girls. And your daughters don't see any affection," Marisa said. Margo sighed and returned to staring out into the horizon.

Margo knew that her sister was right. There was something missing. She and Marius had been pulled apart. She also knew it was very much their own doing. Marriages don't fall apart while the two people are watching idly. She knew there were moments she could have grasped onto her husband and communicated that something wasn't right. She knew she could have been stronger in insisting that he stop drinking. She also knew that he could have done something to bring back the balance in their relationship. She used to respect him. She used to hold him in high standing. And it had nothing to do with how much money he was making. It had all to do with how he made her feel. Marius used to make her feel loved. And it wasn't the kind of awe men tended to present in front of beautiful women. It was the kind of love full of appreciation, gratitude, that you get to spend your life with someone who brings you joy. That feeling disappeared. Her husband, on his best day, presented as a man who felt lucky that he was with a beautiful woman. Yet Margo detested being relegated to nothing more than her beauty. Beauty fades, and she knew that.

"It's not that simple Marisa," Margo said, "I can't just walk away from my marriage like it means nothing," she added.

"Margo, you get one life. That's it. One life, and after that, there is nothing else. So, do you really want to spend it in an unhappy situation? If I was in your shoes, you'd be sitting here telling me the same thing. In fact, you'd probably be plotting how to sabotage my marriage," Marisa said. Margo laughed, because she knew it was true.

Were she the one counseling Marisa on her marriage, she would incessantly try to disrupt the union. Margo was abrasive in a manner that Marisa was not capable of. And the more she thought about it, the more she realized that her sister was genuine in her opinion of Marius and the marriage overall. Though she never hesitated in anything in her life, Margo was wary of making a decision she would later regret. She did not want to put herself in a situation where she would end up unnecessarily blowing up her life, just to chase the rush of intimacy.

"You know that Harry would make a much better partner," Marisa said. Margo giggled.

"Yeah, sure," Margo said.

"Margo, we all know he is handsome and sexy," Marisa said.

"You're not lying there,"

"He is self-employed and uber successful, so you don't have to worry about money. He is well traveled and cultured. He makes you laugh. You know he makes you laugh,"

"That's true," Margo replied despite not wanting to think about him.

"He has this energy about him. When he walks into a room, it's like he brings nothing but joy and happiness and electricity, but the good type. Like the kind of energy that makes you want to be in the same space, you know?" Marisa said.

"Oh, Marisa, you're in love with Harry," Margo said. Her sister scoffed. Then she started to laugh.

"You're crazy Margo. Me and Harry? C'mon you're not being serious," Marisa responded in her veiled attempt at pushing her sister's comment to the side.

"You know I'm right Marisa," Margo said.

"That's nonsense. All I'm trying to do is point out Harry's good qualities. You know he is infatuated with you. You are his forever girl. The one that got away. And you know he'd do anything to get back with you," Marisa said.

"Marisa, you don't have to deny your attraction to Harry for my sake. It wouldn't hurt my feelings," Margo said. Marisa chuckled.

"I'm not trying to protect your feelings. There is nothing between me and Harry and we all know that. I'm trying to help you see that you and Marius are at your breaking point. And lucky for you there is a perfectly great guy who happens to think the world of you, and just so happens to be hot," Marisa said. Both sisters laughed.

Margo thought hard about what her sister said. Harry would be a great catch. He was exciting. He represented the most awe inducing time of her life. But the difference between Marius and Harry was that she knew Marius through and through. While one can never truly know another person, after a decade of marriage, you get to know the ins and outs of their character. They may hide some aspects of themselves, but in general you know who they are. She did not know Harry in such an intimate manner. She knew the guy she dated. She knew the guy she cheated on numerous times. That he is still enamored with her, was exciting and strange all at once. Margo was not the best girlfriend Harry could have had. She did not hide from that fact.

Margo also knew that her sister, despite her protestations, was in love with Harry and had been for a long time. Margo was the more beautiful and outgoing sister. And that did not leave Marisa with room to grow. Most people, mind her closest friends, knew her as Margo's sister. There was no comparing the two. If you wanted to have a lively time, you went with Margo. It bothered Margo intensely that her sister could not admit that she was indeed infatuated with Harry.

Marisa was so used to being secondary to her sister that she learned to put her own needs aside. This was one aspect of their relationship that Margo did not want Charlotte and Emily to share. Emily was proving to be a force of nature much like her mother, but Charlotte was equally daring.

"We all know you never really loved him" Marisa said to break the silence which had befallen them.

"What?"

"Marius, you never really loved him," Marisa answered.

"Pfft...of course I did. Why did you think I married him?"

"Because you got pregnant with Charlotte, or did you forget?" Marisa said. Margo shook her head.

"Marisa, I love my husband," Margo said as she sipped her coffee.

"Sure, you love him now. But you didn't love him then. Time will make you love someone if you are around them long enough," Marisa said.

"That's not necessarily true," Margo said, "and sure, it may not have started with the kind of love you'd have in a fairy tale, but it was love of some kind. And it's grown over time. That's natural," she added.

"Honey, I just don't want you to live with regret. Ten years from now, what if nothing changes and you're still married to Marius? And Harry goes on to marry someone. Are you going to look back and wonder if it would have been better for you to cut your losses? I mean, ten years is a good enough attempt at making something work. There is not going to be a magical change in your relationship with Marius. If anything, things could get worse," Marisa said.

The sisters sat in silence as each pondered what Marisa said. Ten years was a long time in any relationship. And the things that came out of Marisa's mouth could equally have been applied to Marisa herself. She lived most of her life on the outside. It was no secret, though they never talk about it, that Marisa had secretly been in love with Harry. It was no secret that she had also been infatuated with Dorian at one point. Yet time and time again, someone that she loved took action and won the heart of the guy she was interested. First it was her older sister, then it was her best friend Julia.

Marisa's life was one of waiting. As if suddenly the men of the world would discover that she had always been there and would come running to her. She failed to shine the light on herself, always willing to do so for others. This was precisely what she was doing sitting next to her sister. She was shining the light on Harry and making a case for him to her sister, knowing well that she herself loved him. Marisa started to sniffle as she thought about her own life and what her sister had said about her desire for Harry.

She was sad for herself and her inability to attract the attention of the men she was interested in. She thought about the fact that she had been single for a long time, with no real prospects on the horizon. When they were younger, Margo would joke about Marisa becoming a spinster. One of those storied cat ladies, talking to her cats as if they would answer with something of substance. She didn't want that life for herself. Yet she could not see a future where someone would love her the way she deserved to be loved.

"Maybe you're right Marisa. Maybe I'm just fooling myself in thinking that my marriage is going to last forever," Margo said, "I don't know...for the first time in my life I'm actually scared," she added.

"What are you scared of?"

"I don't know...everything? What if Harry doesn't love me when he finds out who I really am? What will happen once he remembers how horrible I was to him in the past? And what about my girls? What kind of example would I be setting for them? I don't know, it's all just too much," Margo answered.

"Margo, I've never known you to be afraid of anything,"

"That's just it Marisa. When you present a strong personality, everyone thinks you can handle anything and everything. But that's not true. It's all a performance. And I'm very good at performing. But sometimes, the fears take over. When I was quitting my high paying job to start the bridal shop, I was scared out of my mind. But at least Marius was working, and it was easier to navigate my fears. Things have just been bad for a while between us, and I just...I really don't know what to do,"

"Well, you know you can always count on your sister to be honest with you. And I don't think this marriage is good for you," Marisa said. Then the girls came running out of the house, Emily chasing Charlotte with a plastic bat. Marisa and Margo laughed as they watched the youngest try her best to hit her sister with the bat, too entertained to intervene.

Later that night, it was a surprise to them both when Margo showed up at Harry's hotel room door. He hadn't expected anyone to visit him and was about to open a bottle of wine when he heard the distinct pattern of three knocks on his door. When he opened the door, Margo was standing there in a sleek black dress, with a small black handbag in her hand. The diamond earrings dangling from her ears reflected the light from the hallway into his eyes. He could hardly speak as he looked at her as if observing a masterpiece at the Museum of Fine Arts. He opened the door a little wider and she walked in, neither of them electing to speak for the moment required little words.

Margo strolled through the modest hotel room and went over to the table by the tall windows and placed her bag down. She leaned against the table, watching as he closed the door and walked in her direction. Harry stopped by the queen-sized bed, fiddling with the sleeve of his pressed white shirt.

"I have to say I'm a little surprised to see you here," Harry said.

"Trust me, I'm equally surprised to see myself here...considering everything I said to you the other day," she replied as she played with the diamond bracelet on her right wrist.

"Marius is okay with you being...here?" he asked.

"Must we talk about my husband?" she asked, "I didn't get dressed so I can come talk to you about another man Harry," she said. He smiled at her. Then she caught a glimpse of the look that always made her feel hot all over. She was feeling that heat now as he looked at her intensely while rolling the sleeves of his shirt.

"My apologies. It's simply the shock of seeing you here, looking as beautiful as ever, Margo," he said. She batted her eyes.

"For some odd reason, I assumed you'd be in the presidential suite," Margo responded. He chuckled.

"Don't think it didn't cross my mind. I simply could not imagine spending that kind of money when I'm in the process of buying a house and leasing an office," he responded.

"So, you really are moving your business here then?" she asked. He nodded. She sighed.

"Does that bother you?"

"No... not at all, it's just..."

"Having me around complicates things for you," he said as he walked over to her. She raised her eyebrows, doing her best not to look into his eyes.

"I never thought you and I would ever...I didn't think we would ever be around each other again. At least not in this way,"

"And what way is that Margo?" he asked as he gently touched her shoulder.

"No, it's not what you think,"

"What is it that you think is going through my mind?" he retorted.

"God, I need a drink," she said and walked over to the little table where he had placed the bottle of wine he was planning on drinking.

Harry chuckled as Margo maneuvered away from him to go to the wine bottle. He could tell that he was making her nervous, and he liked the fact that he was able to have this sort of effect. He wondered how much guilt she had processed before she knocked on his door. It was not unlike Margo to make a rash decision like leaving her husband at home to come see her ex-boyfriend. What surprised Harry was the fact that she showed up despite having told him clearly that she could not entertain his advances.

"Let me open that," Harry said. He walked over to her and she handed him the bottle of wine.

"So exactly what do you do Harry?" she asked as she walked over to the bed and sat down. Harry opened the bottle of wine and grabbed two wine glasses from the cabinets.

"I manage people's money mostly, but I also consult with businesses making strategic changes," he poured wine in the glasses and handed her one, "the guy at the store said this Malbec is one of the finest he's ever tasted," he added.

"Don't they all say that? I think it's part of the wine store employee handbook," she said. He laughed.

"I suppose you're right about that,"

"So, you are good at it then?" she asked as she sipped the wine.

"I'm good at many things. What are we talking about?" he responded. She laughed and almost spat out her wine.

"Harry stop it ...I was asking you about managing people's money and the consulting thing," she asked. He walked over and sat next to her on the bed.

"Yes, I am good at managing people's money. I'm good at helping people make great decisions for their businesses. I've made a lot of money doing that...but none of that really matters when you think about it,"

"What...what do you mean," she said as she ran her finger around the rim of her wine glass.

"I love what I do. I really do. But there is so much that's missing in my life. I always felt isolated. The more money I make, the less connected to people I feel." he said. He was now staring at her.

Despite her attempts to not look at him, she felt his eyes on her. His gaze was focused and unapologetic. It had the sort of intensity that her husband lacked. Her heart started racing as she felt the heat emanating from his body right next to her. She reached out and touched his hand and he grabbed hold of hers. He seemed to be less interested in the wine than he had been before.

"Is that why you decided to come back? Because you were missing something you couldn't find in London, or Paris, or Milan?" she asked. The manner in which she delivered her question gave the impression that were it truly up to her, she would not be living in Oakwood.

Margo longed for a life away from all that she knew. From time to time she reasoned that the edgy teenager she used to be never really died. She detested the manner in which people she knew growing up were content with staying where they were. She admired Harry's decision to go see the world for himself. He had been to places she couldn't have dreamed up. And yet he was returning, back to what he had always known, and to the people who had always been there.

"I like Oakwood. It is not a small town, nor is it a big buzzing one like New York, or San Francisco. But it has its charms. There is connective tissue here," he responded as he took a sip of the wine. She laughed.

"Connective tissue? It sounds like the wine is going to your head Harry," she said. He smiled.

"It's hard to explain sometimes," he said, "but when you are moving around as much as I do, the one thing you yearn for is a place to call home. A stable environment. We all just want a place where people are happy to see us when we walk through the doors," he said as he gently moved her hair from her face and tucked it behind her ear.

"I'm happy to see you," she said quietly, "God, what am I saying?"

"All that is true within you," he said as he leaned closer to her.

When their lips finally touched, Margo felt the hairs on her arms rise as if she was preparing for the biggest scare of her life. She hadn't remembered how soft his lips could be after a few sips of wine. He kissed her as if she were a treasure that he must caress and handle with tender loving care. She in return grasped his face with her hand and pulled him into her, as if they were always meant to be one. And when he released her lips for air, the air in the room never tasted better.

"I don't want to overstep boundaries Margo," he said as he got up from the bed and placed his wine glass on the small table next to the wine bottle.

"I wouldn't be here if I had boundaries," she replied. She hadn't thought much about what was coming out of her mouth. She was captured, in every way possible.

The man standing in front of her didn't have to do much to light the fire within her. She was a willing participant. And as much as her internal voice would remind her that she was a married woman and such dalliances were unfitting of her character, she wanted nothing more than to shut it up, and truly feel alive again.

"Harry," she said as she got up and walked over to him. She placed the glass of wine on the table.

"Yes Margo?" he responded, his eyes fixed on hers. She leaned closer to him, her face passing his as her lips reached his ear.

"Will you make love to me?" she asked.

CHAPTER FOUR

The Letter

A few days later, Harry was returning from a business meeting when the concierge at the hotel stopped him mid-stride. The short rotund man with thinning white hair had a white envelope in his hand. Harry and this man hardly spoke on the occasions they came across one another. Harry was not even sure if he had seen him before. He was certain he'd recognize the white hair if he had seen it before but wasn't sure. The envelope had a stamp on it, but there was no return address on it.

Unable to place whether he had seen the concierge before or not, Harry was wary of accepting the envelope from him. He was not one for conspiracies, but considering the nature of the world, he learned to be careful when accepting things from strangers. Hoteliers were no different than any stranger he'd encountered out on the street. The relationship between any patron and a hotel was innately transactional, and one could not be certain that the workers were fond of him or her. Harry studied the man carefully, paying attention to how finely pressed the white-haired man's clothes were. It was clear this was someone who took pride in his appearance, despite the thinning hair.

He took the envelope from the concierge, being careful not to give away the fact that he did not completely trust him. The white-haired gentleman smiled and nodded as he released the envelope into Harry's hand. Harry smiled in return, placing the envelope in his suit jacket's inside pocket.

"Are you enjoying your stay with us Mr. Melville?" the man said. Harry nodded.

"Yes, it's been quite nice. You guys are stellar...Raymond," Harry responded as he finally read the man's name tag.

"That's wonderful to hear. You let us know if you need anything at all. I will be here until 11 pm tonight so don't hesitate to call," Raymond said as he turned to walk back to the front desk.

"Thank you," Harry said.

As he entered the elevator, he removed the envelope from his jacket pocket. He looked the envelope over multiple times. Then he opened it just as the elevator doors opened on his floor. He thought about how peculiar it was that someone would send him an envelope. He assumed there'd be a letter of some sort, or an invitation to a social event in the envelope. Yet he marveled at the idea that someone would choose to send a physical letter rather than an email as was the norm in this age of mankind.

Inside the envelope was a letter just as Harry had imagined. However, the letter was handwritten. Harry smiled when he noticed it. It suggested that it was of a personal nature. He quickly opened the door to his hotel room and entered. He placed the letter on the table and went to the closet to put his jacket away. Then he opened the letter and sat in the chair at the desk by the window and read the letter.

Harry sat back in the chair and carefully placed the letter back on the table. Then he took a deep breath. He was elated. He could not have done better if he had tried. He had gotten Margo to see the possibility of life with him. He anticipated that whenever it was that she decided to take the plunge and leave her husband, he would feel guilty. Yet as he sat there, looking out the window into the clear afternoon sky, he did not feel guilt. He felt as though what was happening was the nature of two hearts entwined taking its course.

He looked at the time on his watch as he had to meet his best friend Dorian for dinner. It was still a little early and Harry thought about calling Margo to talk to her about the letter she sent him. He refrained from calling her when he thought about what she must be going through after having sent the letter. Harry reasoned that it must have been hard for her to sit down and write those words to him. She loved her husband, even if she wasn't in love with him, and that was not something she'd easily get over.

Dorian was seated and on his second glass of whiskey at the Red Clover restaurant when Harry pulled up to the valet. He fixed his suit jacket and buttoned it as he entered the establishment, met at the door by a spritely young woman in a black dress that stopped right above her knees. Harry had taken to paying close attention to the little details about a person. He noticed that her little earrings were the shape of a water droplet, and that the pins in her hair were brown, much like her eyes. She smiled at him as if it were all part of a performance and he was the audience who must not be disappointed.

"I'm meeting Dr. Carver here. Dorian Carver, that's what the reservation is under," he said. The young woman pulled out a phone from her dress's pocket. He hadn't noticed that her dress had pockets.

"What am I doing?" she asked and laughed, "Dr. carver is already seated. Sorry about that Mr. Melville," she added.

"It's okay. And call me Harry," he responded.

"Thank you, Harry, follow me," she said, and he followed along.

The restaurant, a French fusion establishment with a penchant for gastronomical experimentation, had been open for five years. Harry wanted to frequent the restaurant but could never make time for it during his trips to Oakwood. The decor reminded him of Paris, with obscure wall art that could have been painted by one of the masters of expressionism in their prime. There was the sound of smooth jazz emanating from the walls, giving the impression that a band of real live jazz musicians were playing, hidden in the walls, resigned to their fate of entertaining a wealthy clientele.

"Here you are Harry, I hope you enjoy your experience with us," the young woman said. Dorian got up from the chair and grabbed hold of Harry.

"I thought you were going to bail on me," Dorian said as the two men hugged.

"No, never. I was on a call with a client from Singapore," Harry said. Dorian nodded.

"Always making money huh Harry?" Dorian said. Harry smirked as a well-dressed young man in a dark three-piece suit came to the table.

"I can't help it," Harry said, "I'll have what he is having," he added.

"Yes, sir," the young man said and left.

"So, what's going on? How's your love triangle?" Harry asked. Dorian laughed.

"There's no love triangle," Dorian responded.

"You really should just tell Julia the truth," Harry said. Dorian rolled his eyes and took a sip of his drink. The waiter returned and placed a glass of whiskey in front of Harry.

"What is the truth?" Dorian asked sarcastically.

"That you love her, and you want to spend the rest of your life with her. I mean you might as well propose at this point," Harry said. Dorian laughed.

"You are crazy you know that?"

"Yes," Harry responded, "but I'm not wrong," he added. He and Dorian clinked their glasses together.

"She is so anxious around me Harry. I just don't know if she is really feeling the way I'm feeling. I think part of the excitement for her is nostalgia, but then I'm always wondering if at some point the past is going to creep up in her mind and she'll pull away," Dorian said as he looked through the dinner menu.

Harry understood that Dorian would follow his advice. They had the sort of relationship where he'd lead, and Dorian would reluctantly follow. Harry was the older of the two, by two years. They grew up as brothers and struggled to be away from one another, as if linked, heart to heart. It was due to this deep connection that Harry knew that Dorian and Julia were meant for one another, if Dorian would only see past his perception of Julia's reservations.

"You're kind of a coward," Harry said as the waiter returned, "I'm sorry, not you," he added. The waiter chuckled.

"I'll have the Duck a L'orange with the nitrogen treatment," Dorian said, "He'll have steak, medium well, because he's boring as hell," he added. Harry laughed.

"Will that be it?" the waiter asked. Both men nodded and the waiter collected the menus and left.

"What do you mean I'm a coward? I'm trying to process things. I have to adjust to coming back here and working with both of them. It's not easy," Dorian said. Harry chuckled.

"Yeah, what a hard life Dorian. You have two women who absolutely love you and somehow have convinced themselves that you are the absolute best person they could have in their lives." Harry said.

"You have no idea what a burden that is," Dorian said. Harry chuckled, and then Dorian laughed.

It was while watching his increasingly drunken friend laugh that Harry finally touched his breast pocket and remembered that he placed the letter he received in his jacket's inside pocket. Suddenly his face lit up, much to Dorian's confusion. Harry flashed a reserved smile and dug his hand inside his jacket pocket. His hands emerged with the white envelope.

"Harry, I really don't need your money," Dorian said jokingly.

"No, I'm not giving you money man, I got this today. It's a letter," Harry said.

"Who sends letters?" Dorian asked.

Harry removed the letter from the envelope and handed it to Dorian. Dorian, in jest, carefully opened the envelope and removed the letter. He then carefully opened the paper as if handling a piece of masterpiece art from Picasso's blue phase. Dorian's face looked surprised when he noticed that the letter Harry had handed him was written by hand. He carefully studied the letter, as if trying to see if he could prove that it was some sort of fancy type that looks handwritten. Then he read the letter. Dorian read the letter a few times, as though what was written defied comprehension. He looked up at Harry after the third time reading the letter. Then he looked back at the letter and read it again.

"Wow," Dorian said.

"I know right?" Harry responded.

"What did you do to this poor woman that she is willing to leave her husband for you?' Dorian asked as he handed Harry the letter. Harry shrugged.

"I can't say I have anything to complain about here, but it is a bit gnarly to think that what I had planned in my head is what is playing out," Harry said and placed the white envelope back inside his jacket pocket.

"Have you...did you talk to her yet, about this?"

"No... not yet, but I have to, right? I mean, no one's ever written me a handwritten letter like this before," he said. Dorian nodded.

"That is significant, that she took her time to actually hand write that. I mean she's in love," Dorian said, "I wish someone would write me a letter," he added and both men laughed.

"I thought about calling her when I read it. But then I thought maybe she's been through enough already today after writing and sending the letter," Harry said.

The waiter returned with a runner and placed the plates in front of Harry and Dorian. Both men began to eat, each quarantined into the harbors of their minds, contemplating the meanings of the actions of the women in their lives. While Dorian knew what he had to do and was reluctantly trudging along, Harry's path to love was not as clear. From the letter he received, he knew that Margo was receptive to his advances. Her showing up at his hotel was a sign that she was willing to cross whatever boundaries, both real and imagined, existed between the two of them and bliss. The letter, at the minimum, amplified the emotions she expressed when the two of them slept together. However, there was the problem of her marriage. Had Marius been more of an alpha-male, who kept up the attraction and love between he and his wife, Harry would have felt a sense of responsibility to cast his own feelings aside. The fact that Marius did not make her happy, left room for Harry to pursue Margo, and he loved the thrill of it.

"What are you going to do?" Dorian asked as he paused from taking a bite from the crispy succulent duck on his plate.

"I don't really know yet. I think I'm going to wait a few days to see how things go. I think there is a lot to think about, and I don't want her to feel like I'm pressuring her to make a decision about the rest of her life," Harry responded.

And he was right in his assessment that whatever Margo decided to do, was going to affect her for the rest of her life. Harry was mindful of the fact that walking away from a relationship you invested in and built up over the years was no easy task. As much as he would have loved for Margo to implode her marriage, he knew that the two little girls she woke up to every day would feel the effects of their mother's actions. He wondered then, why he cared so much about the unintended consequences.

"What about you?" Harry asked. Dorian gulped.

"I asked Julia to help me with my house hunt, and it's been interesting interacting with her outside of work," Dorian said.

"That's really good. I'm closing on a house soon too, so we'll have to throw a party of some sort," Harry said. Dorian nodded.

"Yeah...I really love that girl, and I don't want to ruin it...again," Dorian replied.

"And you won't. You just have to be strong enough to let Stephania know there is no place for her in your intimate life going forward. I know how much you care for her, but you know deep down she's not the one for you. Better to let her go than to have her hang on for the long haul only to disappoint her later when she is in love with you," Harry responded.

Though he did not verbalize it, Harry remarked that this was the first time in a long time that the two of them had a conversation about their personal lives that wasn't littered with immature jokes or male-centric posturing. They were both at a crossroads in their lives, that mirrored their professional standing.

"Did you catch that football game last night?" Dorian asked.

"Oh yeah...phew, for a second there, I thought we were going to talk about our feelings all night," Harry responded. Dorian laughed and they clinked their glasses together.

A few days later, Harry was seated at a table in the outdoor plaza of the Main Street Eatery when he noticed across the street, Margo and the two girls come around the corner. Margo was wearing a white dress with spots of small flowers sewn into it. Her dark hair dangled around her ear as she flashed a smile at the girls who were skipping. Then he noticed Marius, not too far behind, trying to catch up to the women in his life. Marius looked tired and worn out. He had a look in his eyes, which suggested he was doing the best he could.

Harry reached for his phone, wanting to call Margo, but then she saw him. Across the street, her eyes met with his. She had a loving look on her face. Her smile was wide, her head turned to the side to hide her longing gaze away from her husband. Harry smiled. He stood up, but Margo shook her head. Marius was closing up on her and the girls. It would not have been difficult for him to figure out that his wife was eyeing the dapper gentleman at the outdoor eatery across the street.

So, Harry sat back down. He'd have loved to talk to her. To mention the letter, she sent. He wanted to find out if she really meant what she wrote in the letter. He was all in, as far as loving her was concerned. Harry hadn't imagined that he'd feel the way he was feeling. Seeing her and Marius together with the girls, playing the happy family, Harry felt a mix of jealousy and guilt. He was jealous that Marius got to call Margo his wife. Though he never saw himself in the role of a doting husband, the idea that someone else got to play that role for Margo bothered him.

Then the guilt fell in. Being aware of the difficulties in Margo's marriage with Marius gave Harry an inside scoop into her mental state. And while he did not balk at the opportunity to take advantage of a struggling marriage, a part of him wondered if Margo and Marius would have a better chance to fix their marriage if he wasn't involved with her.

As the family of three walked by, Harry, who had been sitting again, instinctively got up. However, he turned around just before Marius could see his face. The waiter who was tending to him walked up to him.

"Mr. Melville is everything okay?" the waiter asked.

"Oh yeah. I just need to use the restroom," he said as Margo glanced back just as Marius passed Harry. Marius waved at his wife as though she was looking back at him. Harry smiled at Margo.

"Can I get you more coffee?" the waiter asked.

"Yes please, and thank you," Harry replied as he headed for the restroom.

The next morning, Harry awoke, fired up and energized. And his enthusiasm was not due to the fact that it was the day he was going to sign the contract for the office space he was going to use for work, as well as for the two-story house he was purchasing. The house, he felt, was much bigger than he needed for one person. However, he allowed himself to dream about Margo and the girls moving in with him, should she really go ahead and leave her husband.

As he walked down the stairs of the hotel, Harry thought about the fact that it was both crazy and presumptuous of him to think that Margo was going to leave everything she had worked hard for and bring her little girls into a situation that she couldn't guarantee was going to work for them all. He had the letter in his side pocket and knew that he had to talk to Marisa about it. Marisa was his partner in his endeavor to woo her sister and he needed to talk to her about the letter. Harry wanted to ramp up his attempts with Margo.

As he drove through the streets of Oakwood, Harry marveled at how much his hometown had changed. He felt good about returning home. He imagined that he could play a serious role in the future of the city with his ability to bring in international investors. He even imagined one day running for public office. And to do that, he'd have to have a good presence in the town and affect change in a real way. He particularly thought about bringing new developments to the eastern part of Oakwood that never had real investments like the northwest side where he grew up.

Driving into the hospital parking lot was becoming one of Harry's favorite things to do. He had many friends working at the hospital, but he was excited to see Marisa again. He could count on her to point him in the right direction. As he got off the elevator, he saw Rebecca, Marisa's secretary sit up, her eyes wide open, her fingers toying with the metallic gray shawl around her neck. The older woman, enamored with the sharply dressed Harry, flashed a smile as he approached the desk.

"Rebecca, good morning, you look quite chic today," Harry said. Rebecca batted her eyes.

"Oh Harry, you're making this old woman blush,"

"Old? My dear, you don't look a day over forty," he said.

"Forty? I'd have preferred thirty Harry, but I forgive you for that error," she responded. Harry laughed.

"My sincere apology, I think your beauty has scrambled my brain," he said. She laughed.

"Harry can you stop hitting on my secretary?" he heard from behind. When he turned around, Marisa was standing there with a stack of papers. Harry looked her up and down, taking note of her purple dress with the black belt hugging her waist.

"Don't stare, Harry, ladies don't like that," Rebecca said.

"I'm sorry," Harry said. Harry hadn't taken into account how beautiful Marisa was. She did not look exactly like her sister, and she certainly didn't show off her body the way Margo was known to.

"What are you doing here Harry?" Marisa asked as she walked to her office. He followed after her.

"I can't come see my friend?" he asked. She scoffed.

"You know, most people have to make an appointment to see me. I'm a big shot here you know?" she responded as she put the stack of papers on her table. Harry sat down on a chair across from Marisa's desk.

"I'm sorry your ladyship. I wanted to talk to you," he said.

Marisa sat down on the big chair behind her desk. She crossed her legs and leaned back. He expected her to say something, but she didn't. She simply sat there looking at him, and he stared back. The two of them were at a standoff, waiting for the other to reveal their cards. Then Harry smiled and leaned forward, reaching inside his jacket pocket, he brought out the envelope.

"I'm assuming it's about Margo," Marisa said.

"She sent me this letter," Harry said as he handed her the envelope. Marisa took the envelope and opened it. She read the letter for a few minutes and then handed it back to him.

"That's good," she said.

"What do you mean?" he asked, "wait did you cut your hair?" he added. He hadn't noticed earlier that her brunette hair was cut short.

"Yes, I cut my hair, and it's good that she is ready to leave Marius for you. I think that's a positive thing." she said.

"It looks good," he said.

"What?"

"Your hair Marisa. Looks good. Brings out your face," he responded.

"Thanks Harry," she said as she turned to her computer and started typing.

"What should I do?" Harry asked.

"Harry, I think my sister is in a vulnerable state right now. You have to show her that you care and that you will be emotionally available to her the way Marius hasn't been available to her," Marisa said.

"That simple huh?" Harry asked.

"Harry, when it comes to romance, it's better to be straight forward. Let people know how you feel so that they're not guessing,"

"Is that what you do Marisa?" he asked. She scoffed.

"I..."

"Who are you dating these days?" he asked as he put the envelope back in his pocket.

"That's none of your business Harry Melville," she said. Then there was a knock on the door. "Enter," she said, and Rebecca came in.

"Ms. Hannigan, Dr. Haim's office called. He is asking if you were still coming?" Rebecca said. Marisa sighed.

"Harry, I have to go see this doc really quick. Will you be around or?"

"Yeah, I'll wait. I don't really have anything to do right now," he said.

"Ok," Marisa said and left.

Marisa had been gone for ten minutes when Harry started to get a little antsy. He got off the chair and paced around her office. Then he decided to sit on her chair. Because he had been working for himself for a long time, Harry was not used to being in a lavish office paid for by someone else. He wanted to get a feeling for what that was like. So, he sat in Marisa's chair. He spun around in the chair like a little child being given access to a chair that was much bigger than them.

"Mr. Melville, can I bring you something to drink?" Rebecca said as she popped her head into the room.

"Coffee please, Rebecca," he replied. She smirked.

"Nice chair isn't it?" Rebecca asked.

"Quite comfortable," Harry replied.

"I'll be back with your coffee," she said. Harry nodded.

Harry did not make it a habit of going through people's documents, but he was curious about what Marisa did for a living. So, he started to leaf through her paperwork. And the more he looked at the papers, the more intrigued he was. It hadn't occurred to him before to question what was in front of him. Harry had taken things for granted. This makes no sense, he thought to himself. Something was not right. Had he made a mistake? Was she just being helpful or was she pouring her heart out without having to be direct about it? Harry removed the envelope from his jacket pocket and opened it up. He looked at the letter, carefully studying the lettering, the movements on the page. He paid real close attention to the words used in the letter and the manner in which they were written.

He then picked up a document on which she had written a report. He looked carefully at the document, studying the lettering and the words and the shape of the letters. There was no doubt in his mind. The letter in Harry's possession was not written by Margo. It was written by Marisa. Harry sat back in the chair and took a deep breath. He did not know what to think of what he was looking at.

"Here's your coffee Mr. Melville," Rebecca said as she entered the office.

"Thanks Rebecca...is this Ms. Hannigan's handwriting?" Harry responded as he showed her the document he was looking at. Rebecca nodded.

"Yes, she has a very distinctive handwriting, doesn't she?" Rebecca responded as she placed the coffee cup on the desk in front of Harry.

It was clear then that Margo did not write the letter. Harry got up from the chair as Rebecca left the room. He grabbed the coffee cup and paced back and forth. He couldn't figure out why Marisa would have written the letter. The letter was very personal and gave off the impression that the person who wrote it cared deeply about the recipient. Even if Marisa was writing it for her sister, Harry felt that it was far deeper than any letter anyone would write on behalf of someone else. He was confused.

As he walked back and forth in the room, occasionally sipping the coffee, he wondered if Marisa always had feelings for him, and that he simply did not pay attention to her. He hadn't thought about Marisa in any other way but as Margo's sister. Then he thought that maybe he was overthinking it. He reasoned that it could have been that Margo asked her sister to write her a letter to help her, the same way he was coming to Marisa to ask for help in his attempt to seduce Margo away from her husband.

When the door opened, Harry was startled, almost spilling the coffee in his hand. It was Marisa who had returned from her meeting with the doctor. Her short brunette hair swung across her face as she closed the door and turned her head. She smiled. She was beautiful. He hadn't seen that before. Why was he now seeing her as she had always been? He wondered as she walked across the room to her desk. She looked at him, confused as to why he was staring at her, his eyes fixed on her face like he had never done before.

"She makes really good coffee, doesn't she?" Marisa asked.

"Um, yes, she does,"

"I once had a 21-year-old intern here. She made the absolute worst coffee I have ever had. There is something about older people that brings patience and care to everything they do," Marisa said as she pulled her chair, "hey have you been going through my papers? Those are confidential information Harry, you can't do that, I can get in a lot of trouble," she added.

"I'm sorry Marisa, I got a little bored," he said.

"Anyway, in terms of your situation with Margo, take her out on a proper date. I can play a little interference with Marius and make sure someone is watching the girls, I'm sure she'd love it," she said as she returned to typing on her computer.

"Yeah, that's a great Idea. You're always so helpful Marisa," he said as he placed the coffee cup on her desk.

"Anything for my sister," she said.

"I have to get going now," he said. She got up and walked over to him.

"It's great seeing you Harry," she said and gave him a tight hug. Harry hung on for a few seconds longer than he normally would have.

And when he let go of her, she had a quizzical look on her face. She smiled and he waved goodbye and left her office. Harry was perplexed. His visit to Marisa was supposed to give him a clearer idea as to what he wanted to do next, or what he ought to have done. Yet it simply created another branch on this romantic tree he was climbing. He liked the idea that Margo asked her sister for help. However, a part of him wondered if the letter was Marisa's way of sharing her own feelings without putting herself on the line. He would have liked to have asked her a direct question about the letter and whether she wrote it or not, but he knew she did not like being put on the spot. He didn't want to create an awkward situation between the two of them. So, he figured it would be best to approach Margo regarding the letter.

CHAPTER FIVE
The Heat

Margo had planned things perfectly. From the moment she received a call from Harry that he wanted to have dinner with her at La Cloture, she knew she had work to do to make sure that she was available and that her husband was occupied. Though Marius was not keen on going out anywhere with her, he also never liked the idea of her going out if he was not present. Over the years, she managed to skirt the issue by planning nights out with her girlfriends as a sort of respite away from her husband's constant whining and overwhelming dullness.

Convincing Marius' mother to entertain her son and her grandchildren took little effort. Marla, Marius' mother, often complained that she did not see her grandchildren enough. It is also important to point out that the woman also often complained that Charlotte and Emily were under supervised brats who did not understand the value of a grandparent in their lives. Nonetheless, the girls loved spending time with their grandmother. They loved the fact that they were able to get a rise out of the otherwise stoic older woman with gray hair that reached the top of her coccyx.

As was becoming the norm now, for most of the Saturday, Marius complained about his wife going to hang out with her friends at the expense of family time. He was becoming dangerously good at guilting. She imagined that in his mind he had convinced himself that if he whined enough and played on her heart strings hard enough, she'd abandon her plans and stay home with him and the girls. But what he did not know was that recruiting his mother was done purposefully so that Margo wouldn't have to succumb to the guilt and shame of wanting to enjoy herself away from her family.

As the afternoon came, Margo was alone in the bedroom leafing through her dresses in her walk-in closet. The strapless pomegranate colored short dress had been sitting in her closet for two years and she had not found a decent occasion for wearing it. She assumed she'd wear it on a special occasion with her husband, but given the fact that Marius seemed to have given up on trying to return to the man she fell in love with, Margo resigned herself to never being able to wear it. She could have worn it on any other occasion, but it happened that she endowed this dress that she purchased in a boutique store in Sidney, Australia, with so much meaning that it would seem to cheapen it's value if she wore it for any mundane activity.

Margo pulled the dress out of the closet and held it in front of her as she stood in front of the mirror in the walk-in closet. She did not want to risk putting it on at that moment because she did not want Marius to see her in it. He'd understand that it wasn't her girlfriends that she was getting ready to see. It would be evidently clear that she was getting ready to go see a man. And as she heard footsteps coming up the stairs, she quickly grabbed the bee-striped dress she had eyed as her backup dress and put the pomegranate colored dress back into the closet. The door opened and she smelled the stench of alcohol flowing through the air as her husband entered the bedroom.

"Margo! Mago!" Marius shouted. Margo came out of the walk-in closet with the bee-striped dress in her hand.

"What is it Marius?" she asked, "God, for one day can't you lay off the booze?" she added.

"What? I only had a couple of beers. Jesus can't a guy drink a couple of beers on a Saturday?" he responded. He sat on the bed.

"Marius, your mother is going to be here anytime now. You really need to get ready," she said as she placed the dress on the chair by the bedroom door.

"I don't...I really don't know why you are having my mother come here. I really don't like it when you do shit like that Margo. I'm perfectly capable of driving the girls to her," he said.

"Marius, you think I'm going to trust you behind the wheels with my precious girls in this condition?"

"I'm their father. I deserve even a small amount of trust damn it!" he responded.

"Don't raise your voice at me Marius. You are drunk, and you need to do something about it. I just don't feel safe having you drive my girls," she said as she removed her bathrobe. Marius' eyes alight as he glanced at his wife in her bra and panties.

"God, I've missed you," he said as he got off the bed, "why don't we just have my mother take the girls by herself and you and I stay here by ourselves, spend some time together like we used to before these little monsters came into the picture?" he walked over to her.

"Jesus Marius, I need to get ready. Please go put on a decent shirt, I don't want to hear anything from your mother about me not taking care of you. I'm not your damn servant," she said as she walked past her husband and went into the bathroom. Marius stood there, a dejected look on his face as he stared down at the floor.

When Marla pulled up to the house in her Volvo with her calculated cheery smile, Margo knew that she too had to put on a performance. The two women did not get along when they first met. And over the years, they both learned to steer clear of one another by being overly cordial. As long as Marla did not give Margo parenting advice, Margo was happy to have her watch the girls. Marius would have loved for his mother and his wife to be on better terms, but he could never escape the fact that Margo strongly believed that his mother spoiled him, and he failed to find a mother in his wife.

Margo hugged her girls tightly and then placed them in the car. She hugged Marla with a sideways hug and told her to take good care of her girls. Marius' mother had a displeased look on her face, but whatever she was thinking at that moment, she did not share with Margo.

"I'm sure you're going to talk trash about me with your mother, so enjoy it," Margo said as she hugged Marius.

"Why do you say such things?" he replied as he held onto his wife's hands.

"It is..."

"You look really nice," he said. She sighed.

"Thanks honey," she said and kissed him, "I'll see you later,"

"Have fun, but not too much," he said as he entered the Volvo.

When she pulled up to the front of La Cloture, Harry was standing outside in a three-piece suit. She scoffed as she put the brakes on. It was in Harry's wheelhouse to go overboard in his dressing. Though she thought he looked good, she didn't want to think about how much better he dressed than her husband. The valet opened her door and she stepped out in her pomegranate colored dress, her long diamond earrings dangling above her shoulders. She removed her wedding ring and placed it in her black purse.

"You look ravishing," he said as she walked up to him. He hugged her. He smells so good, she thought as he pulled away.

"You look great as usual Harry," she said.

"Thank you. After you," he said as she entered the restaurant.

The restaurant had a classic decor with chandeliers that brightened the rooms. They were escorted to the bar area first by the maître d' so that he could check and make sure their table was set to his liking. And while they waited, a waiter came up to them with two glasses of champagne.

"Fancy," she said.

"Well, I thought you deserved the best," he said. She smiled.

"So thoughtful of you Harry,"

"Your table is ready Mr. and Mrs. Melville," the maître d' said, "I'm Louis, and if you need anything, feel free to ask," he added.

Margo followed behind a young waitress and Harry walked behind her. She wondered if he was staring at her behind as he was known to do from their dating days. The calming sounds of Bossa Nova filled the room, muffling the sounds of people talking. Margo worried that she might be seen by someone who knew her well, but she didn't want to back out of dinner with Harry. She enjoyed his company, and she wasn't sure how much longer she was going to continue with the charade that was her marriage to Marius.

Harry pulled her chair for her, and for a moment, her heart sank in her chest. She was not used to little gestures of the gentlemanly kind. Her experience with her husband had been so devoid of affection outside of the animalistic need for sex that she had forgotten what it was like for someone to show care in small little gestures.

Margo also understood that the way she was feeling may have a lot to do with the fact that Harry was a different man. He was different in that he was not her husband, whom she had gotten to know thoroughly. He was different in that his baggage were foreign to her. Though she dated him in the past, it was not a relationship that offered the kind of depth that a marriage offers. It was this fact that made her apprehensive about leaving Marius, though she was certain that her marriage had run its natural course.

"I was very excited when you called," she said as she took a sip of champagne.

"I'm glad you agreed. After seeing you the other day, I couldn't help but think about you," he said.

"I guess I should walk across the street from you more often," she said. They both laughed.

"I have to say...the letter...it really touched me," he said.

"The letter..." she started.

"The letter you sent me. I mean deciding to leave your husband is no easy task. I applaud you in how carefully you have considered this. I know it's not easy," he said.

"Yeah, it's not the sort of thing you rush into," she said as she sat up in her chair. She had no idea what he was talking about. It was true that she had been seriously contemplating divorcing Marius, but she hadn't sent him a letter. At least she could not remember sending him one.

"The fact that it was handwritten...it's the small personal touches in this day and age that really capture a heart you know?" he said. She smiled in her attempt to give off the impression that she was fully aware of what he was talking about. She knew then that her sister must have sent him a letter. She herself never would have handwritten the letter, especially when it would have been easier to type it.

"Believe it or not, it is sometimes difficult for me to express how I feel in person...especially when it is about you," she said. He smiled. She loved his smile. Her heartbeat increased as he reached across the table and touched her hand.

"I hope I'm not being too forward in saying that it makes me happy to see you," he said.

"Not at all. I could use a little directness in my life Harry. Honestly, I could use a little of you in my life," she said as she rubbed his fingers.

As the night went on and the more champagne filled their glasses, Margo found herself more and more enamored with Harry. Everything that came out of his mouth seemed to be perfect. His tone was measured, never giving away any sense of a negative feeling, while constantly reaffirming her beauty and intelligence. She wondered how long he'd be able to keep that up. After all, as great as Harry seemed, he did not know her dark side. He may have remembered the young woman who serially cheated on him, but he had not experienced her rage the way her husband had experienced it. In the same vein, she did not know the bad things about Harry, if there were any. The more she stared into his eyes, the more she wanted to believe he was exactly as he seemed. A figure of gentle strength, willing to cater to the woman he cared about. She found herself being removed from her state of trance by thoughts of the impending collapse of her marriage. And every time she teetered on the edge of that voyage down the dark rabbit hole, Harry grabbed her hand and gently rubbed it. It was as if he was synced into her frequency and knew when she needed to be rescued.

"The food here is impeccable," she said.

"As is the company," he replied. Her cheeks turned red as her smile widened. She used her hand and fanned herself.

"You've got to stop saying things like that Harry," she said.

"You'd make a liar out of me?"

"Stop it, I might fall madly deeply in love with you,"

"You mean you aren't already?" he asked. She laughed.

"God, I hate you," she said. He chuckled.

"I don't want this night to end," he said as he looked through the dessert menu. She sighed as she looked at the time on her watch.

"It doesn't have to...at least not yet," she said. She reached out and touched his hand. He looked up at her, his eyes intensely focused on hers. "This was my first time wearing this dress," she said and laughed.

"And I'd like to take it off," he said, "I'm sorry, that was not meant to be said out loud," he added quickly. She laughed.

"I bet. What other dirty things are going through your mind Harry Melville?" she asked. He laughed.

"That's my little secret Margo," he responded.

A little later, Margo was driving while Harry sat in the passenger's seat. He had taken a service car to the restaurant, unwilling to risk driving if under the influence of alcohol. Margo on the other hand, did not have that sort of foresight. Yet she refused to let him drive her car. She did not trust anyone behind the wheel of her precious vehicle.

It was Harry's idea to head to Sawyer's ice cream parlor. It was one of his favorite places. He and his best friend Dorian spent hours there in their youth and worked there in the summers while in college. Margo had no affinity for the place. The times she had been there had been brief and so she had no special connection with it. She would have preferred if they had gone straight back to Harry's hotel to drink some more, but she indulged his desire for ice cream.

"What's your favorite flavor?" he asked as they got out of the car.

"Pistachio," she answered. He started laughing. "What's so funny? Pistachio is a fantastic flavor," she added.

"No, it's not," he said, "no one thinks Pistachio is a fantastic flavor," he added as she chuckled.

"I can't help the fact that I have a more cultured palate Harry," she said as she playfully pushed him away from the door.

The ice cream parlor was sparsely populated. It hadn't changed much. It was the type of place where the owners don't bother adding new paint or refurbishing the furniture, and yet the customers continue to show up. And as they walked up to the front counter, the older woman standing behind it recognized them.

"Harry...Margo... Oh my God, I haven't seen you kids here in over a decade," the woman said.

"Mrs. Olive, how are you?" Margo replied.

"I'm good. Good. Margo, didn't I hear you married that fellow you were dating a few years ago?" Mrs. Olive said. Harry smirked.

"She is very married Mrs. Olive," Harry said.

"And you my dear boy? Anyone steal your heart yet?" Mrs. Olive asked.

"Every day," he replied. Margo blushed.

Margo worried that Mrs. Olive, the owner of the establishment noticed that she was blushing after what Harry said. The fact that Harry was staring at her while talking to Mrs. Olive did not help the situation. She knew that Harry was a little intoxicated, but she didn't want his behavior to betray her attempt at stealth.

"You really shouldn't be so careless," she said as Harry led her to a bench outside the ice cream parlor.

"Are you upset?" he asked. She shook her head as she took a bite of her ice cream.

"No... I'm not mad. I guess it's going to take some getting used to...being in public with you," she said.

"It's harmless...we were friends at one point, weren't we?" he said as he pulled her closer to him. She chuckled.

"Friends? Harry, you and I... we...we weren't friends. You were my very doting and respectful boyfriend," she said.

"I know that..."

"Harry, not to bring up the past or anything, but I wasn't the nicest girl. And you still loved me. That's what our relationship was." she said. She kissed him on the cheek. He put his hand on her lap.

"Well, I like to think we were good friends," he said.

"So, tell me about your new project," she said in an attempt to change the subject. She did not want to remind him of what a terrible girlfriend she was to him. She remembered that they had a great time together. However, she also remembered that she was impatient, and he was immature. She remembered that she found the college age boys more attractive and often sought their company even though she was involved with Harry. These things were no secret. She did not try to hide them. She was perplexed by the fact that Harry chose to either bypass or forget this portion of their experience as a young couple. She'd have thought Harry would hate her for the way she treated him, but Harry was understanding, to his detriment.

"I'm financing a new building in the North East quarter of Oakwood," he finally said before another bite of ice cream.

"Oh wow...how do I buy into this?" she responded. Harry laughed.

"I'm sorry Margo, it's a very private affair," he said.

"What? I thought we were more than great friends? I have some money to invest," she said. Harry chuckled. "I bet you if it was Dorian asking you would make it happen," she added.

"I make it my business not to give investment advice to my friends," Harry said. Margo scoffed.

"Are you ready to head out?" she asked. He nodded.

"Don't be mad at me Margo," he said as he came face to face with her, "I like your smiling face," he said. She pulled him up.

"Let's go Mr. Private affair," she said, "that's what I'm going to call you from now on."

They had been in Harry's hotel room for half an hour when he opened the bottle of Malbec, he had in the small refrigerator in the hotel room's kitchenette. Margo, a little buzzed but still in control of her faculties, was sitting on his bed, leaning back, holding herself up with the use of her hands.

Harry appeared a little more inebriated than she was as he struggled to open the wine bottle. Margo laughed as she watched him struggle.

"The normal thing to do at this point is to offer to help a struggling guy," he said. She laughed.

"Why...why would I jeopardize my own entertainment Harry?" she asked. He chuckled. "Come kiss me," she said.

"I don't have the bottle...It's not open yet Margo," he said. She smiled.

"It has been said that a good kiss can inspire a man to greatness," she said. He laughed.

"No one has ever said that...except for you...right now," he said. She picked up one of the pillows and threw it at him.

Harry managed to get the bottle open and then took a swig from it. This caused Margo to explode in laughter as his performance of barbarism amused her. He flashed a wide silly smile like a character from a comic book and she could not stop laughing. Then he kicked his shoes off and walked over to her. He grabbed her face in his hands and kissed her for what seemed like a long time. And by the time he released her lips, she was gasping for air.

"Are you inspired yet?" she asked. He chuckled.

"Not quite," he said.

"Oh, no, I have failed all womanhood," she whispered.

"You have a very sexy whisper," he said.

"Oh yeah?" she said, again in a whisper.

"I have to say, that letter really touched me. It... It was very unexpected and ...I can't tell you how many times I read it over and over," he said.

Margo was caught off guard by his talking about the letter again. She had not written the letter. She did not know its content, yet he seemed to be so captured by what it contained. She feared that he was starting to fall in love with the idea of the woman on the page he read. Margo was not that woman. Perhaps some part of her was in the letter, but because she did not write it, whatever ideas he was getting, were far from the truth of her being. She grabbed him as he was about to talk again and kissed him. She wanted to keep him occupied so that he didn't linger on the letter much longer. She presumed that she could distract him with her body.

"Oh, Margo," he said. She quickly pulled her dress down from the top, revealing her black brazier.

"Less talking, more pleasing," she said as she buried his face in her chest. Harry could hardly contain himself.

"Be careful what you wish for, I... I can be a monster," he said playfully when she allowed him to breathe again.

"Mr. Melville," she said as she wrapped her legs around him, "do not underestimate my ability to thrill," she added. Harry laughed.

A few hours later, Margo was still thinking about sex with Harry as she drove home. She had sobered up by then, and it was late. As she drove, she vacillated between the exuberance of her lust after Harry, and the dread of going home to see her husband. She looked at the time and it was 1:00 in the morning. She hoped that Marius would have done enough drinking to put himself to sleep as he had done many times before. She did not want to have to talk to her husband while her body was riding high on the intimate time she had with another man.

The more she pondered as she drove, the more it made sense for her to divorce Marius. Harry's presence had unlocked something in her. She felt alive for the first time in a long time. Margo hadn't counted on being so open with Harry. She hadn't thought any man other than her husband would make her feel what she was feeling. But there was doubt in the back of her mind. Though she was confident in what she could offer him and what he could offer her, she feared that Harry was in fact slowly falling in love with the person who wrote him the letter. He was in fact falling in love with her sister, even though he didn't seem to be aware of it.

Marius was waiting on the stoop as she pulled into the driveway. She tried her best to keep a still face so not to give away the fact that she was annoyed by his presence. From what she could see from inside her car, Marius did not look like he had been drinking. This worried Margo. The last thing she wanted was for him to figure out that she had been with another man. She wondered if she had Harry's smell on her. She had sprayed herself with perfume she carried in her purse, but she did not know how well the sage infused perfume masked other smells. Marius stood up when she opened the door and exited.

"Hi honey," he said. She stuffed her purse under her arm.

"Why are you still up?" she said as she locked her car.

"I wanted to see you," he said, "I thought you would have been home a little earlier," he added as he hugged her.

"How were the Brontës?" she asked.

"They were good. They were actually quite good. They only made fun of my mother once tonight," he said. She laughed.

"Well...that is wonderful to hear," she said as she entered the house.

The house was quiet. So quiet that she could hear the girls sleeping upstairs. It was unusual for their house to be so quiet. She couldn't remember the house being that quiet since they started having children. Margo could hear Marius' voice behind her. However, she could not hear what he said. She placed her bag on the table by the couch in the living room and kicked off her shoes.

"I'm sorry Marius, I didn't hear a word you said," she said.

"I said that was not the dress you had on earlier," he said. She remembered then that she had switched dresses. It was a simple slip up, but the kind that could give away more information than she wanted to give.

"Oh yeah, I changed. I thought I looked a little fat in the other dress," she said as she lay on the couch.

"You fat? Stop it," he responded.

"I know...women, you know, we're always beating ourselves up," she said. He chuckled.

"You look really nice in it Margo," he said. She closed her eyes.

"Yeah sure," she said.

"Listen, Margo, I want to talk to you about something," he said.

"Marius, I'm really tired," she said.

She could hear him move around. She kept her eyes closed, feigning sleep so that she didn't have to face whatever was to come. Margo knew from experience that when your partner says they want to talk about something, it usually meant that they caught you doing something and wanted to give you enough rope to hang yourself. She feared Marius found out about Harry and was now going to put her in an untenable position. She could hear him walking away from her and then a few minutes later, he was back.

"Margo...Margo...Open your eyes Margo," he said. She moaned.

"Marius, I'm tired...honey, can we please do this tomorrow?" she answered.

"Margo, please open your eyes," he said. She opened her eyes. In front of her, was her husband on his knees with a big diamond ring.

"Marius...what...."

"Margo, I want to renew our vows. I've been really thinking about it, and with the anniversary coming up soon, I think we should renew our vows in front of all our friends and family." he said.

"Jesus..." she said. She did not know what else to say or do. This was the last thing she wanted. Yet he looked at her with the same loving eyes he had the night they got married. His request, if anything, was going to make life more complicated for her.

CHAPTER SIX
Reluctant Lovers

A month would pass before Margo and Harry would get a chance to be near one another again. The occasion was Harry's housewarming party. He purchased a house in one of the posh neighborhoods of Oakwood's North West quadrant, not too far from his best friend's new house. Not one to be outdone, Harry insisted on having a party to show off his new house, as well as connect with friends he did not get to see often.

The silence between Harry and Margo over the month, was something that happened naturally as the two of them tried to figure out how they were feeling about one another. Harry was not aware of the fact that Marius had asked Margo to renew their vows. It was something that would have affected his thinking. However, he also was not aware of the fact that Margo had delayed giving her husband an answer about the renewal of vows so that she could figure out the best way to tell him she wanted a divorce.

True to his nature, Dorian was the first to arrive at Harry's house. The caterers had brought the food for the night an hour earlier. Dorian did not ring the doorbell. So, when he entered, Harry, who had been trapped in his thoughts about what it would be like to see both Margo and Marisa at his new house, was startled. To the point that he spilled the orange juice that was in the glass in his hand onto his blue dress shirt.

"Jesus Dorian, you couldn't ring the doorbell?" Harry asked as he wiped his shirt.

"You should always be prepared,"

"To be assaulted?"

"I didn't assault you. And also, what grown man drinks orange juice in the afternoon?" Dorian responded as he patted his friend on the head.

A few minutes later, the place was buzzing with guests, mostly people Harry knew as a teenager, and a few acquaintances from his different business ventures. He glanced through the crowd and could not find the Hannigan sisters. Though he was confident they were going to show up.

"Please, say something," Harry said as he stood by the kitchen door watching as his friends Dorian and Julia stared at one another.

Julia was a true beauty, and everyone knew that, but Harry was always careful to never tell her. He had a sort of sibling's relationship with Julia, not unlike the one he had with Dorian. He had been present for much of their tumultuous relationship. And to now see the blossoming of their love for one another, Harry felt pride as if he had something to do with it. He also felt as though he himself would benefit from having the sort of deep attraction to one another that Dorian and Julia had.

"You look absolutely ravishing," Dorian said.

"Thank you," Julia said and took a little bow.

"Oh wow, you're so smooth Dorian," Harry mockingly said. Dorian reached back and hit him on the head.

"I'm going to kiss you now," Dorian said.

"Oh, okay," Julia replied but she could barely finish her thoughts when Dorian grabbed hold of her and kissed her.

"It's like watching my parents make out," Harry said as he closed the kitchen door.

Harry left the two lovebirds in the kitchen and returned to the living room where he was met with loud applause. Harry loved entertaining and loved the attention of others even more. He took a bow and raised his glass to everyone in the room as people paused from eating and socializing to pay attention to their host.

Though the ambience was lively, and people seemed to be enjoying themselves, for Harry, the night had been largely uneventful. An hour had passed, and he had yet to set eyes on the guests he was most excited to see. It was unlike Marisa to show up to any event late. Margo on the other hand was notorious for showing up late, though she did often bring a swathe of excitement and evergreen curiosity with her whenever she entered a room. It was one of the many things Harry found alluring about her. He decided to head to his new home office in the back end of the house to retrieve the letter Marisa had written. He found himself thinking more and more about her since he discovered in her office that she was the real author of the letter that had captured his imagination.

"Oh, c'mon guys, this is just disrespectful," Harry said as he opened his office door. In front of him, Julia was seated on his desk and Dorian was in front of her as the two lovers were kissing.

"Oh my God Harry, I'm so sorry, we'll leave," Julia said, quickly fixing her dress.

"Don't bother, I'm going to buy a new desk tomorrow," Harry responded. Dorian and Julia both laughed as he closed the door to his office. Though he presented as a man annoyed and insulted by the sight of a woman sitting on his desk while swapping spit with her paramour, Harry was actually amused. He loved them, and he would do anything to encourage their growing trust in one another.

As Harry turned away from the door, he was accosted by a blonde-haired woman in a ruby-colored dress with a pearl necklace that quickly drew attention to her ample breasts. Harry stopped short of staring at the woman's chest as she pulled him by the waist. He did not know this woman and could not place where he might have seen her before. Yet, in the interest of being a gracious host, he refrained from berating her for being in his house.

"Oh, hello," he said as they made eye contact.

"I'm sorry Harry, I'm a bit handsy when I drink," the woman said.

"That's alright, I won't hold it against you," he said, "do we know each other?" he answered. He wondered if he had dated her before or perhaps, she was a one-night stand, he could not remember.

"No, we don't, but I'm hoping to change that," she said, "I'm Debra Schloss, from Schloss and Partners," she added.

"Oh," he said. He gulped. "You're Martin Schloss' daughter," he said. She nodded and revealed a big wide smile.

Martin Schloss was the developer of the project Harry was investing in. He had heard of his daughter, but never met the woman. Though he found her attractive, Harry was wary of entertaining the idea of her, as he did not want to mix his business affairs with his personal life. She was still holding onto him as he pondered a way out of this predicament. Martin Schloss, as he remembered, was a man with an irritable temper.

"I guess your father couldn't come tonight," he said. The woman nodded.

"You know dad's always busy chasing the next dollar," she said. She finally released him. She moved her hair about so that he could get a clear look at her face.

"Well, welcome to my humble little space," he said. She laughed.

"Humble? It's an impressive house Harry," she said.

"Thank you,"

"So, what is the state of your bachelorhood?" she asked, "I mean that's what all the women here are really interested in if you don't mind me being frank," she said. He chuckled.

"Well, I am involved with someone," he said. She had a sad look on her face.

"Well that's a problem," she said as she grabbed his hands and squeezed them. "A man like you should be free to roam." she added. Harry sighed.

"It's a good problem to have. I think I've done enough roaming to last a lifetime," he said as he slowly released himself from her grasp.

"I see, Harry, I see...well I look forward to getting to know you. I will be spearheading the project for my father so you and I will be seeing each other a lot," Debra said.

"It's a pleasure to meet in person Debra," he said as he shook her hand. She grabbed hold of him and hugged him tightly and then kissed him on the cheek. He was a little apprehensive, but he had to be careful not to offend her. He did not like to deal with family members of his business partners, but he learned to condone certain things to make sure he gets the outcome he most desired.

As he was making his way away from Debra Schloss and her thinly veiled attempt at seducing him, Harry noticed that Margo and Marisa had entered the house. As usual Margo was wearing a dress that stopped short of her knees, revealing her smooth long legs. Her hair was pinned up, leaving her face open. Harry loved seeing that face. Marisa on the other hand, always doing her best to hide, was wearing loosely fitting jeans. Her short hair occasionally flipped into her face, forcing her to have to fix it.

Harry couldn't understand Marisa's discomfort with herself. He thought she was beautiful. He hadn't always looked at her in any meaningful way, but now he could not un-see the beauty. He was confused about his own feelings regarding the sisters. His love for Margo was deep rooted, with elements of time and trial to flesh it out. While his admiration for Marisa was quickly turning into an infatuation with no clear sign of a destination.

Margo jumped when she saw him walking towards them. She pushed past the man they were talking to and gave Harry a tight hug. It was as if the month of absence had grown her attachment to the idea of being with him. Marisa stood by, watching as her sister fawned over the man who was not her husband.

"Careful Margo, it's not like you're married or anything," Marisa finally said as she noticed some of the guests staring at Margo and Harry.

"Oh, get off my back Marisa. I'm just happy to see Harry. That's all. Why can't I be happy to see Harry?' Margo said.

"Hi Marisa. Have you guys been drinking already?" Harry said as he hugged Marisa.

"I'm afraid so," Marisa said, "my wonderful sister insisted that we go out for drinks before coming to see you," she added.

"Well I'm very happy to see you guys here. I thought for a second you were going to ditch me," he said as he put his arms around both sisters.

"I seriously considered it," Marisa said.

"Oh, stop it. She's so grumpy all the time. I just don't get it," Margo said.

"Is Julia here?" Marisa asked, bypassing her sister's judgement.

"Yeah. Last time I saw her she was making out with Dorian in my brand-new home office. So disrespectful," Harry said.

"Oh great. Then tomorrow she's going to want to talk about her feelings," Marisa responded, "every time she and Dorian do something physical, I have to listen to her talk about how she felt about it," she added. Harry laughed.

"It's just down the hall," he said as he pointed out in the direction of the office.

"So, I'm here, you have to give me a tour," Margo said.

As they walked throughout his brand-new house, Margo held onto Harry's arm like lovers do on a promenade overlooking a body of water. He could not have asked for anything more from her. In his presence, Margo seldom mentioned her husband or thought about the troubles in her marriage. Harry wondered if she felt any guilt about what they were doing. He himself often thought about the morality of his involvement with Margo. He did not want to hurt Marius, but time taught him not to ignore his own feelings for the sake of another.

Harry did not go into any scenario half-hearted. He poured himself into everything he did. It worked out for him in the end if he brought his passion into a situation. And as he and Margo walked, and he talked about each room and what he wanted to do with it, he felt closer and closer to her. It was as if there were no obstacles in their way. Yet in the back of his mind, he knew that his burgeoning attraction to Marisa would have to be addressed sooner or later. He could not ignore this feeling he was starting to have. Above all else, Harry wanted to have the sort of all-encompassing love that he saw between his friends Dorian and Julia.

"God, I've missed you," Margo said as they entered his bedroom. She quickly closed the door and pushed him against it.

"I've missed you too," he said and kissed her.

"Harry..." she started and kissed him. Then she bit his lower lip.

"Yes, Margo?" he asked and kissed her neck.

"Harry, just seeing you turns me on so much. I haven't felt like this in a long time," she said. She started to unbutton his shirt.

"Margo...we can't do that right now. I have guests...I have guests in the house. I can't disappear..." he said as she continued kissing him.

"Harry...I'm ovulating...I want to have your baby," she said. Harry chuckled. He did not mean to make light of what she was saying, but he did not think it was a good idea.

"Margo, you're drunk," he said.

"That may be true, but I want to have your baby," she said as she pressed her body against his, "touch me Harry, touch me,"

"Margo...It's not a good idea. Considering the fact...you're still married, Margo." he said. She put her head against his chest and sighed.

"God...I feel like you're holding that against me," she said as she wrapped her arms around him.

"I'm not Margo. I'm not. I just don't think you having my baby is a good idea. It...it would complicate things for you in a major way. You know that." he said. She took a deep breath.

"I know."

A little later, growing weary of engaging with all his guests and wanting a moment of reprieve, Harry headed for his new home office. He was careful to knock before opening the door, so not to be surprised by any guests who wanted to take advantage of the privacy the office provided. When he opened the door, he breathed a sigh of relief that no one was making out in there, or worst, having sex on his brand-new desk. In the left corner of the room, on a heavy wooden chest, was Marisa who had also wanted to get away from the crowd for a moment. She quickly stood up when he entered, as if he caught her doing something she wasn't supposed to be doing.

"I'm sorry," she said.

"What are you sorry for?" he asked.

"Huh?"

"I said what are you sorry for? Were young doing something in here?" he asked as he headed for the desk.

"No… I don't know why I said that. I think I'm a little drunk. I just needed to sit down for a second. I can't keep up with my sister," she said.

"Please sit-down Marisa. No one can keep up with that sister of yours," he said and chuckled.

Marisa nodded and then slowly lowered herself to the chest and sat back down. Harry went behind the desk and sat on his chair. He pressed a button and the chair reclined. Marisa had a surprised look on her face. He nodded.

"You didn't know it could do that did you?" he asked. She shook her head, "and it's so comfortable," he said as he put his feet up.

"I could have been comfortable this whole time?" she asked. He nodded.

"C'mon, come sit here. Take it for a spin," he said.

Marisa got up and walked over to the chair. Harry moved off the chair, returned it to its upright position and motioned for her to sit. She sat on the chair, leaning back a little and closed her eyes. Harry pressed the button on the side and the chair reclined. She took a deep breath and smiled. She put her feet up on his desk, her eyes still closed as she tried her best to relax. Harry proceeded to slowly remove her shoes, trying not to disturb the moment of calm she managed to achieve while sitting in the chair.

"I'm sorry, I didn't mean to put my shoes on your brand-new desk," she said as she opened her eyes.

"Seriously, don't worry about it," he said. He sat on the desk in front of her, her feet next to his leg.

"It's a really nice house Harry," she said. He smiled that bright alluring smile of his as he looked at her and her cheeks started turning pink. She too smiled, a little too hard. Her face started to hurt. "What?" she said and looked away from him.

"I wanted to ask you something," he said. She looked back at him. Harry ran his finger along the bottom of her feet. This tickled her and she retreated her feet a little. He laughed.

"I'm very ticklish," she said.

"Did you write that letter?" he asked. She scoffed.

He was certain she wrote the letter. Even if he hadn't seen her handwriting while in her office, the fact that Margo seemed not to know anything about the letter gave away the fact that she didn't write it. Harry could not conclude factually that Margo hadn't asked Marisa to write the letter, but he was confident in his assumptions. Marisa wrote the letter. He was sure of that. Why she wrote it, he could not tell. Why she did not tell Margo she was sending the letter was even more strange.

"My sister tells me you have some secret big project coming up and you won't let her invest in it," she said as she put her head back. Her hair slid back away from her face as the light in the room shone on it.

"Why are you trying to avoid answering my question?" he asked. She chuckled.

"Why are you trying to avoid talking about your project Harry?" she asked. They both laughed, "I think I'm sober now," she added as she sat up in the chair, putting her bare feet down onto the floor.

"Marisa," he said as he pulled the chair toward him. They were now face to face. "Did you write that letter?" he asked. His stare was unnerving, but she couldn't remove her eyes from his. He himself could feel the discomfort of having stared deep into someone else's eyes. It was not something he did often with the women in his life. He feared they'd figure something out about him through his eyes.

"Yes Harry Melville, I wrote that letter," she finally said. She did not flinch. Her gaze was stern and unapologetic.

"But why?'

"I was trying to help my sister out," she said.

"Bullshit,"

"You don't have to believe me Harry. But I wrote it," she responded, "your floor is very cold," she added.

"Did you mean what you wrote?" he asked.

"Every word of it," she responded. He squinted. She finally blinked. Then she smiled. It was the kind of smile meant to break the ice between two people. It was also the kind one shares to hide one's own feelings.

"Are you in love with me?" he asked. She scoffed.

"Oh, Harry," she said as she started looking for her shoes.

"Don't," he said as she tried to get up from the chair, "don't run,"

The door to the office opened. It was Margo, leaning against the wall. Harry looked behind him to see her staring at he and Marisa. At first it seemed as though she could not figure out who was in the room. Then a few moments later her eyes opened wider. From afar the sounds of Bruce Springsteen's I'm On Fire was heard coming out of the stereo system. Far behind Margo, Harry could see Dorian and Julia dancing among a crowd of other dancers. Margo started laughing wildly. Marisa found her shoes on the floor by the chair, next to Harry's feet. She picked up her shoes and moved the chair back. Then she walked by Harry, barely looking in his direction.

"Harry, and Marisa. Marisa, isn't Harry so goddamn handsome?"

"Sure sis," Marisa responded as she put her shoes on.

"You know, everyone thinks Dorian is so hot, but Harry, now that is charm in a perfect package. So sexy," Margo said. She put her hand in the way as Marisa tried to get by.

"Margo, I've got to pee really bad, so move out of the way," Marisa said. Margo laughed.

"God, my sister is so crude, isn't she?" Margo said, looking at Harry. He shrugged his shoulders. "What were you two up to in here by yourselves?" she added. Marisa scoffed.

"Talking about you, naturally," Marisa responded. She pushed Margo's arm out of the way and left the room.

"She's so testy," Margo said. She took a few steps forward and stumbled a little. Harry rushed to her aid, catching her before she could fall. "My hero!" she exclaimed as she touched his face.

"Should I call you a cab?" he asked.

"What? No, the party is not over Harry," she said and kissed him on the cheek.

"Margo, you've been drinking a lot," he said. She scoffed and playfully punched him on the cheek.

"What's your deal today? You're berating me about drinking,"

"I'm…"

"You won't have sex with me, and you're in here hitting on my sister," she said. Harry shook his head.

"Margo, I'm not berating you, and I wasn't hitting on your sister. We were just talking. I was showing her how cool my new chair was," he said, "look come sit on it, see it for yourself," he added as he brought her over to the chair.

Harry sat her in the chair and stood behind the chair, slowly putting her head back onto the headrest. He then pressed the button that caused the chair to recline. As he looked up, across the room, he could see Marisa standing by the door. Margo's eyes were closed as she tried to get a feel for what the chair was like. Marisa had a sheepish smile on her face. Then she gave Harry a slight wave, as if to concede to his earlier assertion that she was in love with him.

Marisa quickly left, closing the office door as she went. Harry felt as though a moment had been lost. He had been so enraptured in his infatuation with Margo that he never imagined that her sister might have been pining for his attention. She had never given him any clear signs that she might have been interested in him. His history with Margo made it easier for him to be drawn to the more outgoing larger than life sister. Marisa never crossed his mind. But now she was all he could think about. Even with Margo sitting on the chair in front of him, he wanted to be nearer to Marisa. He was confused by his own feelings.

"Harry," Margo said as she finally opened her eyes. She looked up at him.

"Yes Margo?"

"I'm going to divorce Marius. I am. I promise you that," she said as she grabbed hold of his hand.

"I don't want you to feel like I'm pressuring you to do something you don't really want to do. I know you've built a whole life with him,"

"I know. I know. You would never pressure me. And truth be told, I needed you in my life to push me toward something I had always been thinking about. I love Marius, and that makes things hard. But I haven't been in love with him for a very long time," she said. She swiveled the chair around to face him. "I need to do this. It's not about you. He and I just are so far apart. And the way…the way you make me feel…I mean I feel alive when I'm around you. You make things feel easy," she added. She got up from the chair and kissed him.

CHAPTER SEVEN

Detente

The walk to Dorian's house must have been a mile, Harry thought as he walked down the street Sunday morning. He was dressed in shorts, a dark gray shirt and tennis shoes. It was an outfit he had not donned in a long time. Due to his line of business, Harry learned over the years that presentation was everything. As his mentor once told him in his economics class in college, business is a bit like seduction. People say they want one thing, but they want something completely different. It is up to the person doing the seducing to bring the true feelings to the fore. Therefore, Harry always looked nice when he stepped outside.

On this day, he was going over to his best friend's house for breakfast. As he walked, he thought about the fact that Julia would be there, and he would get to have a woman's opinion on his dilemma. Ever since Dorian and Julia reconnected, the two of them became inseparable. Harry did not think their strong pull toward one another would last long, but he had been proven wrong. He had doubts because Dorian always had one thing to his advantage. He was an impossibly good-looking guy. He was the sort of man a woman would compose if you gave her a sketching software and asked her to design a man. Though Dorian did not lean on the fact that he was good looking, it did not keep other women from fawning over him. When they were younger, Harry loved spending time with Dorian, because it meant they would naturally be approached by young women. While the more serious Dorian paid little attention to his surroundings, Harry picked up the signs of interest. They balanced each other out.

At his core, Harry wanted to develop deep love with someone. He spent years living his life like a fleeting bachelor, moving from one place to another, developing business networks, breaking a few hearts along the way. What he was searching for, he couldn't find in just any woman's bed. That was one thing he had realized towards the end of his stint in London. After seeing so many bodies lying next to you in your bed, you start to wonder if there is more. He was convinced there was more, because he had seen it in the relationships his friends were building while he was sowing his wild oats.

Now, having found himself between the two Hannigan sisters, Harry felt trapped. It was an entrapment of his own doing. He never should have approached Marisa about helping him, he thought as he turned the corner onto Dorian's block. He would have been better off not knowing that the younger Hannigan sister had feelings for him. He never would have explored his own feelings about her. Harry was not even sure at this juncture how he felt about Margo. He was drawn to her in a visceral animalistic manner. Margo came with a lot of energy, especially of the sexual kind and he loved it. But then he wondered if she was in any way differentiated from the other women of his recent past. Or perhaps she was just his kryptonite.

He stood idly on the steps having rung the bell multiple times. Harry was patient, and he knew he had to be. After all, he hadn't called in advance to let Dorian know he was coming by. A minute later, he could hear someone walking to the door. When the door opened, Julia was on the other side, her curly blonde hair barely staying in place as she hung onto her bathrobe. Her eyes seemed to shine when met with the bright lights of the sun. He couldn't tell if she was happy to see him or not.

"You really should call before showing up to people's house," she said in a dead even tone. Then she squinted her eyes like a child wanting to berate a friend without using words.

"Please, I do not need to call before coming here," he replied. Then she started to remove her bathrobe in a slow methodical manner. Harry covered his eyes. "Jesus Julia, cut it out. The last thing I want is to see you naked," he said. She laughed and punched him in the abdomen. When he opened his eyes, she was wearing blue shorts and a white tank top. Harry chuckled.

"You're so gullible Harry, come in before the neighbors think I'm giving a free show out here," she said, and he entered. Julia kissed him on the cheek.

Harry could smell pancakes as he followed behind Julia who had thrown the bathrobe on a chair by a mirror in the hallway. Dorian was in the kitchen making pancakes. He gave Harry a slight head nod when he saw him. Harry went and sat at the dining table across from Julia.

"Dorian can you please tell your future wife here to stop giving me trouble about not calling before coming?" Harry asked.

"Hey! Don't give him any ideas," Julia said. Dorian smirked.

"Julia, Harry is welcome here whenever he feels like it," Dorian said as he continued cooking.

"Julia, I was hoping you'd be here actually," Harry said.

"Oh yeah? Why is that?"

"Marisa," Harry said. Julia smirked.

"Oh, I figured," she said. She sat up on her chair and crisscrossed her legs.

"So, she wrote me this letter, as her sister,"

"How do you know it was her?" Julia asked. But Harry had a feeling Julia already knew about the letter and the fact that it was written by Marisa. Julia and Marisa were best friends, it would have been strange for her not to have told her.

"Because when I went to talk to her about it, I noticed that the handwriting on her paperwork in the office was an exact match,"

"Did you ask her about it?" Julia asked.

"Julia, you know that I did. You guys talk so I know that you already know." he responded.

"Harry, Marisa has been in love with you for a long time dear," Julia said, "You've just been so stuck on Margo that you haven't ever seen her," she added.

"I've seen her...I just never thought that she was...interested in me," he said.

"Well, she'll never come after you. She's partial to her sister and she would never do anything to mess that relationship up. Her sister is like a goddess to her," Julia said as Dorian joined them at the table. She pinched Dorian's behind as he walked by her.

"You guys are disgusting, just so you know," Harry said. Julia laughed.

"Does my unapologetic lust make you feel uncomfortable?" Julia asked.

"It was rude, making out in my brand-new office. You owe me a new desk," Harry said as he sliced into the well buttered pancakes in front of him.

"I'm sorry about that bro. We should have been more respectful," Dorian said as he sat next to Julia. Julia shot him an annoyed look. Then she flashed a smile.

"You better be careful with her Dorian,"

"If I show up dead one day you know exactly who did it." Dorian said. Julia playfully smacked the back of his head.

"Hey, that's not nice. You're hurting my feelings," Julia said.

"You have no feelings," Harry joked, and she tossed sliced strawberries in his direction which he dodged.

Talking to Julia confirmed what Harry suspected that Marisa was in love with him and had been for a long time. What he couldn't put his finger on, was how he felt about her. He was intrigued by her, and to some extent was starting to develop strong feelings for her. Yet, he felt as if he'd be playing the role of a villain should he insert himself between the sisterhood of the Hannigan women. Margo, he reasoned, would never forgive him or her sister if he pursued Marisa. However, he wondered if it would be fair for him to ignore his feelings for Marisa simply to appease the married Margo.

But there was another reason why Harry hesitated in the full embrace of his developing emotions for Marisa. It was fear. Fear that his connection with Margo could never be severed. At least not in the manner necessary to give room for a fruitful exploration with Marisa. As much as he'd have liked to think he could easily move on from Margo, Harry knew that there was a chance that his feelings for Margo would linger. This, he believed, would constantly threaten whatever he might be capable of building with Marisa. And for a moment, as he ate his pancakes, Harry wished he could whisk himself out of the lives of the Hannigan sisters. If he could let go of them, and them of him, he figured everyone involved would be happier. Margo would not need to divorce Marius, and Marisa would get the chance to find someone who would love her the way she deserved.

Across town, Margo nervously washed every single dish they had used for breakfast, before putting them in the dishwasher. Charlotte and Emily ran upstairs after eating to video chat with some friends from school. Marius was still at the kitchen table, nursing the coffee in his large coffee mug.

Margo wanted to blurt it out, but she thought it might be unbecoming of her. She had yet to change out of her nightgown. She smirked when she thought about the fact that marriage had turned her into her mother. When she was single, and even when she and Marius first started dating, she wouldn't have been caught wearing a nightgown. Now, she saw the practicality of wearing one, even if it sapped away any hint of sexuality, she might have within her. She hated that her life turned out the way it has. She wanted more, and she was convinced what she wanted, was out there, waiting to be grasped.

"Are you okay? Are you cold?" Marius sliced through the thickness of the silence in the room.

"Huh? What?"

"Are you okay? You look cold," he said.

"What? No, I'm not cold, I'm okay," she responded as she finished putting the dishes in the dishwasher.

"Margo, you're shaking. Maybe we should close the windows," he said. He got up and went to the window and closed it.

He was going to make it hard for her, she thought as she watched him close the windows. He was trying, she thought. But she didn't want him to try. They crossed the bridge already. There was nothing left. The love that pushed them together, the one that came with a force when Charlotte was born, that love had withered away. And they let it. Embracing those feelings was a strange thing for Margo. She loved the freedom that came with the sort of unconstrained self-expression of her early twenties. Marriage, and monogamy, had killed a part of her. And the more she looked at him, the more she thought that he had killed a part of her, and she resented him for it.

"Isn't that better already?" he asked. Little did he know that her shaking had nothing to do with the temperature in the room.

"Marius, I'm filing for divorce," she said as he returned to his chair and grabbed his coffee mug. He stopped, as if he didn't hear what she said, or was trying to run her sentence through a filter to better grasp the severity of her statement.

"What? Margo, what are you talking about? Divorce? You and I are in this for life honey," he responded and chuckled.

"No, I'm serious Marius. I'm really serious. I'm filing for divorce and I didn't want to surprise you with it," she said. He took a step towards her and she backed away as if she feared being attacked.

Marius stared at her befuddled. It was as if he had been hit by a heavy metal truck. He could barely talk, though his mouth seemed to move. He carefully put the coffee mug down on the kitchen table. Margo, showing her resolve, was no longer shaking. She dried her hands on the red hand towel hanging by the drying rack next to the kitchen sink. She could feel Marius' stare behind her, burning through the icy wall between them. He started walking towards her. Her instinct was to flinch, and back away from him, but she didn't. He grabbed her hand.

"Margo, I don't think you mean what you are saying," he said. She shook her head vehemently.

"I do Marius. I mean it. I mean every word of it. This is not a joke. This is not pretend. I'm not happy, and neither are you. And it is not healthy for our girls to see their parents in this state. I'm filing for divorce and that's it," she said.

"Margo, you're unhappy, and I get it. And I'm willing to do anything to make things better. That's why I wanted to renew our vows. I will do anything for you. I love you, you know that," he said as he pulled her towards him.

"No! It's too late Marius. It's too late. And you reek of alcohol, for God's sake. When was the last time you took a shower?" she responded. She released herself from his grasp. "Marius, it's too late,"

"Please Margo, I'm begging you. Please don't do this. Don't blow up our lives," he said.

"For once, I need to think about myself Marius," she said. Marius got on his knees.

"Honey, please don't do this. I'll change. I'll go to rehab; I'll get a job. I'll do whatever it takes. Please don't leave me," he pleaded.

Margo knew that she couldn't stand there longer. It was within her to be forgiving and to filter her decisions through the prism of other people's feelings, even though she portrayed a hard exterior. However, she had to be strong. She made up her mind and she did not want to budge from it. She looked down at him, and it was easy to dismiss his feelings. Marius looked desperate. He had no respect for himself, she thought. She thought he looked pathetic and unworthy of love. It was easy for her to bypass her protective emotions. He was not the man she married and loved and wanted to spend the rest of her life with. He was a shell, and whatever that shell was made of, did not appeal to her.

"I'm going to take a shower," she said as she walked by him. Marius was on the verge of tears. She had not expected this sort of reaction from him. She thought he was naive. Things between them was not going well. He had no reason to expect that she was going to continue being with someone who had nothing to offer, emotionally or sexually.

Margo did not expect there to be any peace in her house since her announcement to Marius about wanting to divorce him. At the very least, she expected him to continue pleading with her, and to even get others involved, primarily his intrusive mother. And while she washed her body, she thought about the freedom that would come with escaping her dreadful marriage. But there was also a sadness that befell her.

The ending of anything substantial takes time and can be soul crushing. She knew that. She had ended things before. Affairs, relationships, friendships, these were all within her wheelhouse. Ending a long-term partnership, especially one in which children were involved, was not something she imagined she would experience in life, but she was at the doorstep now. And she did not want to turn back. The prospect of Harry was a strong draw towards releasing herself from marriage, but it was not the only thing driving her. She missed her old self. And she did not want to continue to resent herself for having made the choice to marry Marius. When she opened the bathroom door and walked out into the bedroom, she was thrown aback to see her husband sitting on the bed, with her computer in front of him.

"What are you doing with my computer?" she asked. It was a question that she didn't need to ask. She knew what he was doing. It was what she herself would have done if she were in his shoes.

"So, this is it huh? This is why you're coming to me about a divorce?" he said. He sprang off the bed and before she knew it, he was in front of her. She held on tightly to her bathrobe.

"What...what are you talking about? What are you doing with my computer?" she said.

"Oh, just getting acquainted with your back and forth emails with Harry that's all. Did you want to talk to me about that?" he responded. She was speechless. She had not thought about what would happen if he discovered her affair with Harry.

"I..."

"So, you go on and have a full-on affair, and then come to me with this divorce as if I was the one doing something wrong?" he asked. He was now right in her face. She could smell the rage emanating from his body.

"Marius, please step away from me. You are scaring me," she said.

"Scaring you? I'm, scaring you? You slept with another man! How am I supposed to feel about this Margo? Has he been the one putting these ideas into your head? He's the one who's convinced you to divorce me?" he said.

"No," she said. Her voice quivered as she attempted to get around the fact that she was having an affair behind her husband's back.

"So just because he makes a lot of money and is well kept, you felt the need to destroy our marriage?"

"Oh, honey, you did that already," she said. His face was quickly turning red.

"I did? I did? So I lost my job and it's been hard for me lately, that's not equivalent. That's not..."

"He's a better lover Marius. He just is. He pays attention to my body in ways you never have. I get excited about seeing him," she said, cutting him short. Now he was speechless. She had upended the upward trajectory of his anger. Now he was hurt. He balled his fist. Margo started crying. "I'm sorry Marius...I'm sorry, but that's the truth," she said. She touched his face.

"You've...you slept with another man...how could you? And this whole time I thought I was the bad guy in this scenario...and you let me believe that," he said. She rubbed his cheeks with her hands. Marius hit her hand away.

A few hours later, Harry pulled up to the front of his house, dejected. He had just gotten a call from Margo. She was sobbing. He wanted to go to her and console her, but he knew that his presence at her house would not have been the best thing for everyone concerned. She explained to him how Marius went through her emails and found their correspondence and deduced that they were having an affair. Though he did not regret having engaged in an extramarital affair with Margo, he hated the fact that the discovery put her in an untenable position. Even though she decided to divorce her husband, whatever leverage she might have had in the proceedings was now erased.

Harry took a deep breath and exited his car. As he walked to the front door, he called Marisa, wanting to talk to her about his conversation with Margo. But Marisa did not answer. Harry was not surprised by Marisa's not answering his phone call. He had also put her in a strange position. He left her a message about her sister, insisting that Marisa go see Margo because she needed to talk to someone who would really listen rather than judge her.

As Harry entered his house, he felt the wind rush hit him. He didn't remember leaving any windows open, but there was a possibility that he did. He walked into his kitchen and checked the windows and one of the windows was open. Harry closed the window and placed his phone on the kitchen counter. Then he walked upstairs to his bedroom, intending to take a shower. When he opened the door, Marius was sitting on his bed. Harry was surprised by the sight of the surly husband of his paramour on his bed. The two men stared at each other for a moment. Harry did not know what to say.

"How did you get in my house?" Harry finally said. Marius rubbed his chin, as if calculating his next move.

"So... this is where it happened, huh?" Marius said.

"Where what..."

"Where you and my wife made love Harry...surely you're not that thick Harry!" Marius said.

"I don't know what you are talking about," Harry responded.

Harry knew that there was no way to eschew the truth in this matter. What he wanted was to stall so that he could figure out what to do. He left his phone in the kitchen, so it wasn't easily accessible for calling the police. But he also knew that threatening the husband of the woman he was having an affair with wasn't the smartest idea. Love can and does make people do stupid things, and Harry did not want to find out the extent to which Marius was capable of doing stupid things.

"You're really going to stand there and make a fool out of me?" Marius asked. He continued rubbing his chin.

"I think you need to leave, otherwise I'm calling the police," Harry said. Marius sprang up to his feet and revealed a revolver. He pointed the gun at Harry's head.

"Go ahead pretty boy! Call the police. That would be ideal. They can come find your corpse. Let's see Harry boy, who is faster? The guy with the gun? Or the guy who has to run downstairs to get his phone?" Marius said as he walked toward Harry.

It was clear to Harry now that Marius was both capable and willing to raise the stakes. Marius was desperate. He was losing his wife and he couldn't take it out on her. Harry was the interloper in their relationship. To him, it made perfect sense to go after Harry. And as Harry stood there with the gun pointed at him, he thought about how he hadn't predicted that the rather docile computer programmer Margo was married to, had more bite to him than anyone could have imagined.

"Harry, you seem to have lost your ability to talk!" Marius shouted. The spit from his mouth hit Harry in the face, making him flinch. He was not prepared for that.

"Look...Marius, right?"

"Oh, he knows my name. How wonderful," Marius said. Harry couldn't help but stare at the revolver. He had to find a way out of the situation.

"Why don't you put the gun away and we can talk. Man, to man," Harry said. Marius laughed.

"You would like that wouldn't you? Do you and my wife think I'm some sort of chump that you can just walk over? Is that what you think? You think I'm just going to sit around while you continue to humiliate me?" Marius asked.

"Look man, I know..." Harry started, but Marius moved in closer and put the revolved on his forehead.

"Get on your damn knees," Marius said.

When Harry hesitated, Marius shot a round into the ceiling. Harry quickly got on his knees. For a moment, he wondered if he could win a fight with Marius. Marius was tall but he was not physically fit. But Harry did not like uncertainty. He did not like uncertainty in business and he certainly did not like it in his day to day life. It would not be out of the question to try and tackle Marius and disarm him, but Marius had the advantage. He had the gun. And at any moment, that gun could go off. And Harry noted from the way Marius held the gun firmly while he shot into the ceiling, that this was someone who was used to shooting guns. The worst thing Harry could do then, was to try and pry the gun from the hands of someone who was not an amateur with a gun in his hands.

"You're going to stop giving me the run around Harry!" Marius said.

"Look man, I don't know what you want from me," Harry said.

"I want you to stop pretending you weren't having an affair with my wife Harry! I want you to own what you have done. Own the fact that you have ruined my marriage," Marius said.

"I didn't ruin your marriage," Harry said, Marius hit him across the face with the back of the gun, drawing blood.

"Wrong answer boy scout!" Marius said as blood dribbled onto the dark wooden floor. Harry's head suddenly felt a mounting pressure as if it was about to explode.'

"Damn it. Man. you're asking for what you don't really want to know," Harry said. Marius lifted the gun again, "don't hit me again," Harry pleaded.

"You tell me what I want to know, and I will briefly consider sparing your life," Marius said. Harry chuckled. "What's funny Harry? Am I not hitting you hard enough?"

"Oh, you're hitting me hard. I'm just wondering how it is that I got myself into a situation involving a guy with a gun," Harry said as he wiped his mouth.

"Have you been sleeping with my wife?" Marius asked, once again pointing the gun at Harry.

"Why are you asking a question you already know the answer to?" Harry responded. Marius kicked him on the side of his abdomen. When Marius' foot connected with his body, it felt as though his bones were suddenly being crushed together. Harry fell to the floor, holding the side of his body in agony.

"So, you think it's okay to bring another man's wife into your house?"

"I... I never had sex with Margo in my house," Harry responded as he picked himself off the floor. "I took her to a nice hotel," he added. Marius kicked him again.

"You think this is funny, don't you? You think it's funny making light of my marriage?" Marius asked.

"I think it is funny that you...you're channeling all this anger towards me. You know...after all these years...I would have thought you'd understand by now that Margo can't be made to do anything she doesn't want to do," Harry said. He winced as the pain proved to be more pronounced than it had been.

Harry was dumbfounded by the fact that Marius couldn't accept what was in front of him. Harry may have had some machinations of his own regarding his play for Margo's heart. But he knew Margo well. He knew that if she didn't feel the sense of possibility, she never would have acquiesced to his suggestions. That he and Margo were having an illicit affair, was a direct result of the fact that Margo wanted to have an affair. Harry couldn't force her hand if he wanted to. It was her strong unrelenting personality that Harry found most endearing about her. And he imagined, it was the same thing that drew Marius to her in the first place. The more he thought about it, as he struggled to get himself up, the more Harry realized that he and Marius weren't that different. He could easily have been Marius, but for the nicer clothing and the respectable profession. Margo had a type, and neither one of them had a choice in the matter.

"I could very easily blow your brain off right now," Marius said as he pointed the gun at Harry's head, "I could end it all right now," he added. Harry rubbed the side of his body.

"Please don't shoot me," Harry pleaded. He was still on his knees, balancing himself by putting one hand on the ground. "I admit, I've been having an affair with your wife, that you are correct about," he added.

"I know...I already knew that," Marius responded. The rage deep in his eyes was evident to Harry as he thought about a way to escape his ordeal.

"What you don't know is the fact that no one can keep Margo," Harry said.

"What did you say?"

"Margo and I used to date, and what you're feeling right now? The feeling that everything is lost, and she just couldn't care, I've been there before..." Harry said.

"Why should I care? Why should I give a damn?"

"Margo doesn't know how else to love," Harry replied.

Though he did not believe that Marius was believing what he was telling him, what he said was the truth. Margo did not know any other way to love but the tease of chaos. She was a sort of tornado working her way into the lives of others, paying little attention to the carnage she leaves behind. And as the words flowed through his mind, Harry finally realized what had been at the top of his mind. Margo, as beautiful and elegant as she was, was not a good person. She was fundamentally flawed and unrepentant. And he loved everything about her. That is why it had been difficult for him to accept the basic truth that her love came with a cost. It took the barrel of a gun pointed at his head for Harry to finally see, to love Margo, one had to despise oneself a little.

"Everything was fine before you showed up...You ruined everything,"

"Man, you're so naive. I didn't do anything but present her with an alternative," Harry said. Marius moved closer to him. "Man, if you are going to shoot me, just go ahead with it. But let's stop kidding ourselves here. You stopped being the guy she married. You dropped the ball, and refused to get back up," Harry added.

"Shut up!"

"You did. You stop being who she loved," Harry said, though he could not say with any certainty that Margo loved Marius. "You want to shoot me? Fine. But that's not going to solve your problems. You're just creating new ones. Think about your girls,"

"Shut up! Stop talking!" Marius said. Harry could see the tears in his eyes.

"You want to leave your girls without a father? Is that really what you want? I understand you love Margo. I get it. I know how that feels like. I know what it is like when she makes you feel like you can have the whole world. But she also knows how to tear you down. She's really good at that.... Marius, you don't want to do this. You know that," Harry said. Marius had a glassy-eyed look on his face. It was as if he had been transported elsewhere.

In that moment, Marius did not look threatening. He looked like a directionless man. He looked as though he did not know what to do. What Harry hoped, was that Marius would come to the conclusion that he did not need to kill him. He did not need to take an action that would completely alter all their lives for the worst.

"You shoot me, you will never get to see Margo again. You will ruin your connection with your girls. You will become the very man you never thought you'd be. That's not what you want, Marius," Harry said. Marius took a step back.

"I love her," Marius said quietly, as if he were the only one in the room. "This is not how things were supposed to work out," he added.

Marius took a few steps back, as if it had suddenly occurred to him that killing Harry was not in his best interest. He had a look of horror on his face as he tried to grapple with the situation, he found himself in. Harry, getting the feeling that he had appealed to Marius' better nature, took a deep breath. A sigh of relief followed when Marius suddenly stormed out of the bedroom. Harry collapsed onto the floor, his face and his body felt as though he had been run over by a truck.

When he managed to get himself downstairs, his hands shook as he dialed for the police. He came to the realization as he was speaking on the phone with the police about what had taken place, that he very well might have been getting in the way of Margo's happiness. He was selfish in thinking that Margo needed him to be happy. Harry imagined that Margo could be happy with Marius. He thought this because he saw for himself just how much Marius loved her. And while her husband may not have been in the best shape she would have liked, Harry did not see himself being able to risk his freedom for her.

CHAPTER EIGHT
Letting Go

It was a rare occasion in Harry's life that allowed him to take note of his own growth. He embraced his feelings. He didn't fear loss. In this way he separated himself from other men. And now he had to see his own growth once more. He had been changing for a while, though he seldom noticed.

The sirens going off as the police surrounded the area, put him at ease. Marius couldn't change his mind now and decide he wanted to kill the man whom he blamed for the disintegration of his marriage. And as Harry sat on the floor of his foyer, he contemplated his ideas of love. They were not so different from those that led Marius to break into his house with a gun. Love had a drunken effect. The more enamored you are, the less likely you were to see what was in front of you. Love will lead you to staying with someone even though you know the person is not good for you. It confused you about where you were going in life.

Harry had been confused, and a bit cowardly. This was what he thought of himself. He was cowardly in that he could not face the fact that the sort of love that came with Margo would leave him desperate, much in the way it had affected Marius. The difference between both men was that Marius was deeply invested and was going to follow Margo in whatever direction she wanted to go, even if it meant him being hurt as a result. Harry was no follower.

He was cowardly in that he struggled to accept the fact that Marisa loved him. She had been careful not to show her feelings to spare her sister's. But he had to have seen the signs, he thought. The way Marisa looked at him, was intense. There was a light in her eyes that suggested a welcomed sight.

The sounds outside got a little louder as he heard police officers shouting at Marius. The beleaguered man had not gone far after all. Harry opened his front door and stepped out. Marius did not put up a fight. He was done fighting. In fact, from the sunken look on his face, he was done with everything. The officers handcuffed him and put him in the back of a car. Then an officer walked over to Harry's house.

"You called it in?" the officer said, taking note of Harry's bleeding face.

"Yes," Harry said.

"I just need a statement," the officer said. Harry opened the door wider as he watched the police car drive away with Marius in the back.

"Please come in," he said and walked inside the house. The officer followed behind him.

"Is he an acquaintance of yours?" the officer asked.

"No, his wife is," Harry responded. The officer smiled.

"I see," he said and wrote down on his notepad.

Harry was determined, a few hours later to get out of his own shell. After washing his face and doing his best to make it look like he hadn't been assaulted, he put on a suit and got in his car. He felt it necessary to confront the situation with Marisa. While she was hesitant to explore whatever speck of interest there may be between the two of them, Harry wanted to face it. He knew there was every possibility that Marisa would reject him. In fact, he was certain she would reject him. The bond between sisters is powerful. Harry knew that Marisa would hold onto her bond with her sister and refuse to explore with Harry in any meaningful way.

He waited in the car outside her house for a few minutes. He needed courage. He had never felt nervous like this before. Yet he was nervous. His heart rate was increasing with every minute spent in the vehicle. Harry started laughing. He could not believe that Marisa made him nervous. Harry did not remember feeling this way towards Margo. Margo was easy to talk to. Her seductive ways were welcoming. You always knew where you stood with Margo. She didn't hide anything if she was interested.

When he pressed the button, he listened as the bell rang throughout the house. It seemed to travel in every direction as if there was an army of people inside waiting for his arrival. Then he started hearing footsteps. But they weren't just one person's footsteps. She was there with someone. Harry hoped he was not interrupting her time with someone she was seeing. He hoped that the second footsteps he heard did not belong to a paramour he'd have to compete with. The door opened slowly, and Marisa peeked her head out to see who it was.

She was wearing a mustard yellow dress. He noticed that she did not have shoes on, and her hair looked as though she had just been woken up from a nap. She looked at him with a perplexed look, moving her short hair to the side as if its presence was an unexpected interference. It was evident that she was confused by his presence at her door. They hadn't spoken in a while so it would have been alarming to see him there. At least that's what he said to himself as she looked at him.

Harry smiled. He hadn't noticed before that she had a nose ring. He tried to remember if he had seen it before. All the times he saw her in her office, he didn't see a nose ring. Even during their more social interactions, he hadn't noticed the nose ring. It fits her face, he thought as his eyes carefully studied her face.

"Harry, what happened to your face?" she asked.

"Um..." he uttered and then couldn't come up with the words to finish his sentence. He had forgotten for a moment that he had just been assaulted by Margo's husband.

"Are you okay?" Marisa asked. Then Harry noticed Margo coming to the door. It was then that he remembered.

"Marius happened to my face," Harry said.

"Oh my God, come in, you probably have a concussion," Marisa said and opened the door for him to come in.

"Harry, what are you doing here? What happened?" Margo asked as she walked up to him and hugged him.

"He said your husband attacked him," Marisa said.

"What? When?" Margo said.

Marisa pulled Harry by the arm and took him to the kitchen. She then opened her freezer and brought out an ice pack. She put the ice pack on his face. The cold ice against his bruised face created more pain than he anticipated, but he did not want to wince in front of the sisters. She poured him a glass of water.

"Where is Marius now?" Marisa asked.

"In police custody," Harry replied.

"Margo you need..." Marisa started. Margo vigorously shook her head.

"I don't need to do shit," Margo said.

"But he is your husband" Marisa said. Margo shook her head again.

"Soon to be ex-husband. And he can rot in jail for all I care," Margo said. Harry drank the water. "God, I can't believe he did that to you. Harry I'm so sorry. He is such a petulant child," she added.

She too was a petulant child though Harry was reluctant to tell her that. Margo as always, was leading with her self-interest rather than what might have been the right thing to do at the moment. Her presence ruffled Harry. He hadn't come there to talk to her, but to reveal himself and his inner feelings to Marisa. At the very least he wanted to reveal the conflict within him as it concerned the sisters. That it took the assault for him to think seriously about Marisa, was problematic, but Harry knew that you had to start somewhere. And sometimes the starting position isn't always as important as the landing place.

Now there was the obstacle of Margo inadvertently placed in front of him. He was not prepared to face her. And he didn't quite know what to do or say at the moment. He held the ice pack to his face. Trying to drum up the courage to say something. He knew not what to say, but he had to qualify his presence somehow.

"Margo, you know I'm no fan of his, but he is the father of your children. Please go get him out of jail," Marisa said.

"Forget it Marisa. He can sit in jail. Why would he do such a stupid thing?" Margo replied, "I'm not going to let him ruin our trip," she added. Harry did not know what Margo meant by trip. So, he figured him showing up was interrupting something the sisters had planned.

"Harry please say something. She's not thinking straight," Marisa said.

"Margo..." he said as he walked over to her. He grabbed both of her hands.

"Oh Harry, I'm so sorry." she said as she rubbed his hands.

"Margo, I'm sorry too," he said, "I've been thinking about this for a few days and I just don't know how to say it. And I think what happened with Marius was a better illustration than anything,"

"Harry what are you talking about? What are you saying?"

"You and I can't be together," Harry said.

It was as if he were Atlas and relief had finally been provided in a swift and decisive manner. He could feel his chest lighten up as he had carried much of his worries about what to say to her coiled up in him. Margo was stunned. She looked as if she was not present. She heard him, but the words seemed distant as if someone else was yelling them at her and she was failing to capture the message.

"Harry, I understand that what you just went through was traumatic. I get it. Anyone who has gone through something like that would start to question everything. I get it, but this is not the time to make rash decisions like this, okay?" she said. He smiled and her face brightened.

"Margo, what happened today didn't get me to thinking about this. I've been thinking about it for a while. It just took me having a gun in my face for me to realize I've been hiding this whole time," he said. She shook her head.

Margo could be stubborn. Harry knew that. She once insisted on fighting a traffic ticket when she was clearly guilty of speeding. Harry happened to be in the car with her as she argued with the police officer to show her proof of her guilt beyond a reasonable doubt. He was embarrassed by the episode. Not least because the end result was him having to bail her out of jail for aggressive behavior. He smiled as he thought about that moment, because the decision he was making, meant that there would be less of those enthralling moments with Margo in the future. It was a moment of letting go of the beautiful full of life woman he always imagined he'd end up with. But Harry now had to admit that the Margo he built up in his head could never be. The woman in front of him, despite her hard shell and her attempt at appearing ruthless was afraid. He could feel her pulse racing. She was afraid, not only of losing him, but of losing the life she built with her husband.

"Margo, you have to go back to your husband. You have to reconnect...you know, when I was staring up at his gun, I could see the despair in his face. You mean everything to him,"

"He means nothing to me now," she said.

"You say that, and maybe it is true. Only you really know what you're going through. All I'm saying is that the years the two of you have spent..."

"Harry stop...please stop, you're upsetting me," she said and hugged his body. She put her head on his chest as she sniffled. "I don't want to think about what you're saying to me...I don't want to think about him," she added.

Letting go never feels like freedom initially. Regret is invariably meshed with decision making. But for Harry, love requires the sort of sacrifice that comes with walking away from a good thing, to find the better thing. He hadn't always felt guilty about his involvement with married women. In fact, Margo was not the first married woman he had an affair with. She just happened to be the one he had the deepest connection with. Shared history made the attachment that much more severe.

Harry did not struggle to walk away from his past trysts. He struggled to let go of Margo, because he loved Margo. He always had. And even as he stood there with her head on his chest, he wondered if he was making the right choice. It was then that his eyes finally met those of Marisa's, who had been standing there in the kitchen listening. Her deep brown eyes watered as she witnessed her sister's dire attempts at holding on to a man who was not hers to have.

If he had never learned to communicate through his eyes alone, this was the time to pick up the habit. And so, Harry looked into her eyes, unwilling to look away. And she too kept the connection, even as tears fell from her eyes. Harry couldn't understand why Marisa was shedding tears. Her mouth did not open. There weren't going to be any words or sounds coming out of her mouth. She empathized with her sister. It was admirable, but Harry knew it meant that Marisa would push back against any ideas he had about exploring his growing infatuation with her.

"I'm sorry, that really hurts," Harry said as Margo squeezed him. He had not shown them his bruised ribs and back.

"Oh," she replied. She slowly lifted his shirt to reveal the black and blue all over his torso. "Harry, I'm so sorry that bastard did this to you. He's such..."

"He's still in love with you Margo. That's all. That's what this was about," Harry said.

"Do you want some Ibuprofen?" Marisa asked as she wiped her eyes. Harry nodded.

Harry freed himself of Margo's grasp and went into the living room and sat on the leather couch. He leaned back as his pain was more pronounced than he had anticipated. Marius did kick him really hard. Marisa returned a minute later while Margo was roaming the hallway talking to herself like a person on the brink of losing their mind.

"Here, take this. It should help with the pain," Marisa said as she extended her hand to him. While reaching for the pills, Harry grabbed hold of her hand, gently. He looked into her eyes and she looked away from him.

"Thanks Marisa," he said in a soft voice.

Marisa had been ambivalent about the way Harry changed his voice to match any occasion. She especially hated it when he spoke softly because it was disarming. Even if one wanted to dislike him, Harry had a way of structuring his words and his voice to make you feel at ease. A conversation with him came with none of the anxiety that can sometimes accompany human interactions.

"Let go of my hand Harry," she said as it finally occurred to the two of them that he was still holding her hand. Margo rushed to the couch.

"Harry…I'm so sorry that this happened to you. I don't know what's gotten into him. But please…please don't let this one event make you think that you and I can't be together," she said.

She's going to make this difficult, Harry thought as he tossed the pills in his mouth and washed it down with a glass of water Marisa had given him. Both sisters, near him, almost looked like they could be twins. The difference between the two of them now was that Margo, the one who seemingly had everything and more in life, looked the most desperate of the two. Marisa was poised as usual, unwilling to let her emotions unfurl in the manner that her older sister's emotions were breaking apart.

"Margo, I'm glad that this happened. And I think you ought to be as well," he said.

"No…no, no, please don't say that. I don't want to hear that," Margo responded.

"But it's the truth. You knew it was always going to be difficult. And I feel terrible that I came between you and your husband. I… I'm sorry Margo,"

"Stop! Harry, I don't want to lose you. I can't lose you," she said and lunged herself at him, crashing onto his pained body. Harry winced as his bones felt as though they were being smashed once more. Marisa, disgusted by her sister's desperate behavior, grabbed the glass of water and quickly walked back into the kitchen. Harry followed her with his eyes, wanting to get up and go to her, but unable to move due to Margo's body latched onto his own.

Despite his reservations about his presence once he found out Margo was at the house, Harry stayed for another thirty minutes. He would have liked to have left earlier, but Margo was in no mood to let him go. Deep down, he understood that in her mind letting him leave the house was akin to letting him leave her life forever. Whatever little moments they were going to have now, would have to last them for a long time. He had disconnected emotionally from her. He did not understand then why that was. It was as if he had suddenly grown a conscience and decided his role in her marital turmoil was dangerous, and unfair.

When he managed to convince her that he really had to leave, Margo let go of him. The physical separation was wrought with emotional distress for all in the house. Margo had to contend with the end of her affair, and Harry had to figure out if it was possible for him to make amends. For Marisa, it all meant that she had to figure out if she was strong enough to admit her feelings towards Harry. It was evident from the way his eyes often wandered to her, that he was not going to hold back in his pursuit of her. He was a sort of hunter in the animal kingdom and capturing her would be an enjoyable effort for him. She did not know if she wanted to be hunted.

"You really should go to the doctor, or the ER. You might have broken ribs," Marisa said as the two of them stood in her foyer. Harry walked towards her, and she took a step back. She'd wanted to resist, but when his hands touched her face, she felt a rush of blood flow through her body to her genitals. And when his lips touched hers, it was as if some invisible hand had shot her with a bolt of electricity. And when he finally pulled away, she simply stared into his eyes. Her mind scrambled, looking for the right words to say, but she could not grasp them, despite reaching with maximum effort.

"Thank you," he said.

"Please don't tell my sister," she finally said and stepped away from him.
"It can't be helped," he said.

"Yes, it can. It must. My sister means the world to me. And she's madly in love with you Harry. We can't do this. we...Please don't ever kiss me again," she said as she pushed him towards the front door.

"Marisa,"

"Please Harry...if you care about our friendship, don't say anything to me that's going to have me thinking about you for days. Please don't. For my sister's sake. Just don't" she said as she opened the door and gently pushed him out.

Harry looked at her once more with those unflinching eyes of his. He said nothing and left. She would think about him, whether she wanted to or not.

CHAPTER NINE
Resistance

Two days later, Harry woke up with excruciating pain in his abdomen. He had been bandaged up by the physician but refused to take the narcotic medication prescribed to him for fear of becoming addicted. During this time, there was no shortage of phone calls from Margo, who seemed to be struggling with the idea that her affair with the dapper businessman and former paramour was now truly over. She even offered to come take care of him, making light of the fact that her husband was still in jail and her little girls needed looking after. Even Marius' mother had called Harry. She did not have the money to bail her son out of jail. It was one of the few times in Marius' life that his mother could not come to his rescue. The mother begged Harry to drop all charges against her son, reasoning that Margo's misbehavior and lust after other men was what drove her son to do what he did. The conversation was brief, but not brief enough for Harry to avoid the consternation of now having to consider the feelings of an old lady trying to salvage her son's increasingly broken life.

All these issues were inconsequential as far as Harry was concerned. It was the day he had planned to put up pictures in his house. And as he sat up on his bed, on the verge of tears due to the pain, he wondered how he would manage to get the pictures up on the wall without causing himself further harm. He would have loved to have been able to call Dorian for help, but the young doctor was out of town. And so, Harry called Julia instead.

He had barely managed to make his way downstairs when his doorbell rang. Julia, more energized than usual, stormed through the doors, patting him on the head as she walked by him. She headed to the kitchen and turned the coffee machine on.

"Julia thank you so much for coming. I didn't expect you to be able to take off work to come here," he said. She shook her head.

"No, it's okay. I have the next two weeks off. It's no bother," she said as she filled the machine with coffee. "How are you doing?" she asked. He smirked.

"I take it you've heard all about this situation," he said.

"I might have,"

"Julia don't be coy with me. We are friends. I can handle it," he said.

"Well, to be frank, you're an idiot," she said. He smiled and walked over to the kitchen table and sat.

"I know. And I'm trying…"

"She really has been in love with you. And you can't think for a second that she's ever going to feel secure with you,"

"And why not?" he asked.

"Because you were just so taken with her sister. I mean, that's kind of cold Harry," Julia said as the coffee dripped. "But I'm not here to beat you over the head for what you've found yourself in. I think you've got some work to do to prove to her that she's not just your next task," she added. She grabbed two mugs and poured coffee in them.

Harry was taken aback by Julia's strong words. It made sense, but he did not want to admit to it. Julia herself had to contend with Dorian's murky dance with another woman in order to get him back. And she would not want her friend to have to go through the same thing. What Harry felt he failed to convey was that his feelings for Marisa were genuine. While Margo's larger than life energy tended to make people attracted to her, it was more a result of lust than it was of real love. Everyone wants to be with Margo because they know they will never be bored. She had that kind of invisible power. She made life interesting. One could not simply figure Marisa out. She had to be unearthed, if she gave you the time of day.

An hour later, as Julia finished putting up the last few pictures, there was a knock on the door. Then the bell rang. Harry, who was holding the last frame in his hand looked at Julia, almost as if this was her house and he didn't know if he should answer the door or not. Julia had a perplexed look on her face. She moved her blonde hair to the side, away from her eyes and motioned for Harry to get the door.

"Are you expecting someone?" she asked.

"No, I don't think so," he replied. He opened the door and was met by Marisa. She was in a business suit. She looked different, he thought, in the work attire. She looked like a different person. Confidence seemed to ooze from her.

"Hi Harry, can I come in?" she asked. Her voice was clear and sharp. There was no hesitancy. She came with something on her mind and she would get her point across. He worried that he might not come out of the interaction intact.

"Marisa, hey honey, what are you doing here?" Julia exclaimed as the two women hugged.

"Just came by to talk to Harry that's all," Marisa said, "God I love your hair, Harry isn't Julia so beautiful?" she added. Harry nodded. Perhaps she was nervous, he thought. People tend to jump subjects when they're nervous.

"I just helped Harry put up some pictures. I was just about to leave," Julia replied.

"Oh," Marisa said.

"Yeah I have to go spend time with my mother. Apparently, that's a thing we do now," Julia said. They laughed.

"Thank you so much Julia. I owe you a bottle of wine," Harry said. Julia kissed him on the cheek.

"Behave yourself," she said like a mother warning her child before he had the chance to misbehave.

Harry walked Julia to her car, and after another stern warning to be the best version of himself, he returned to the house. Marisa was sitting on the couch, her arms crossed, a cold look on her face. The warmth that had just filled the house in Julia's presence was now gone. In its place was a distant chill that threatened to overtake them.

"Would you care for a cup of coffee? I'm going to have another," Harry said.

"No, thanks, I had some earlier," she replied.

In the kitchen, Harry took out a small mirror from a kitchen drawer and looked at himself. He wanted to make sure there was nothing on his face. He rolled his shoulders as he poured the coffee in his mug. If he knew anything for certain, it was that there was going to be a performance in the living room. Marisa, he thought, would do her best to remain distant and cold so not to get wrapped by his charm. He had to do his best to draw her out. It was a task he was more than willing to undertake.

"I don't want to take up too much of your time Harry," she said as she sat up on the couch. Harry came over and sat next to her.

"I have all the time in the world," he said.

"I'm going to need you not to do that," she said as she turned her body to face his.

"Do what?"

"Say things that are going to make me not want to leave...and I have,"

"You don't have to leave," he said. She smirked.

"Harry, please don't be difficult," she said. She looked away from him for a moment. He could see her eyes well up. She was having a hard time, that he could see. He hoped he was not the source of her sorrow, but he couldn't be so naive to think she came there simply to talk to him about someone else. Harry knew why she was there. She didn't have to say much more than she already had.

He'd have been surprised if Marisa hadn't shown up at his house. He went to her house to unload what was on his mind to her. Her sister's presence forced his hands more than he wanted. It was natural that she'd come to him. The strangeness that was between them could easily turn into love, but not without having to break Margo's heart. Marisa exhaled, the heavy air flowing from her lungs into the living room.

"Harry, you are a wonderful guy. I think...I think the world of you," she said, her voice breaking as she spoke. "But we can't...you and I just can't be. We can't. I can't do that to my sister," she added. She abruptly stood up from the couch, regaining her composure.

"Marisa, tell me how you really feel," he said. He leaned back on the couch, giving her the semblance of power that she needed at that point in time.

"Margo is my sister. And it doesn't matter if she divorces Marius or not. I think the two of you are so good together. I can't imagine you with anyone else, let alone me," she said as she paced back and forth.

"I didn't ask you how you felt about Margo. How do you feel?" he said. She stopped and took a deep breath.

"Harry, for God's sake, don't ask me such an inconsequential question," she said.

Marisa left the living room and went into the kitchen. Harry stayed seated on the couch. He couldn't understand why she was unwilling to consider her own feelings. Marisa's devotion to her relationship with her sister was admirable. She was a sort of servant to Margo's causes, but failed to fill her own glass, even when offered the opportunity.

When she returned from the kitchen, Marisa had a glass of water in her hand. She unbuttoned her suit jacket and stood in front of Harry. Harry, starting to feel the pain in his body again, smiled at her, doing his best to mask his discomfort. He did not want her to think she was the cause of his discomfort.

"Harry...I think you should drop the charges against Marius. I think what he did was horrible, and he really hurt you. I get that, but I think if you really care about Margo, you should help her out in this manner. She'll never do it herself. She is far too stubborn to see how this is going to hurt her girls. They're already interrogating her about where their father is. You should do this. I can't do it. She has forbidden me from meddling," she said. She drank the entire glass of water in one fell swoop.

"Yet here you are," Harry said, "meddling"

"I don't know, that's just what I'm really good at," she responded.

"I think what you're really good at is avoiding questions that make you feel uncomfortable," he said. She scoffed.

Harry slowly stood, using his hands to push himself up. He winced as the pain in his ribs reminded him that he was in no position to pretend to be physically imposing. And as he took steps towards her, she stood in place, frozen, as if captured by the essence of the handsome man standing in front of her. Harry took small steps towards her, being careful not to appear aggressive. His mind was alight with thoughts of wanting to make her happy. He had never felt that way about someone before, not even Margo. He truly wanted to see Marisa happy, much more than his own visceral desire for her body and mind.

When he reached her, it seemed as though he had been walking for an eternity to reach the source of all life. There she was, standing with the glass in her hand, unmoved. Harry touched her cheek, running his smooth hands against her face. The expression on her face was like that of an animal stuck between deciding to accept its fate or fleeing. He hoped she wouldn't flee. He couldn't handle that sort of unfiltered rejection now that he was willing to expose himself. He pulled her face gently towards his and kissed her. Their lips sealed one another's mouths and they stayed connected, each letting go of what little resistance existed so that the moment could bloom like flowers in the springtime.

For a moment, and just that, a moment in time where nothing else seemed to matter, there was equilibrium in their hearts. Harry, wary of his own feelings, felt full. He was full of life like he had never been before. He was used to feeling like he was missing something. He always had something to reach for. But right then and there, for the first time, it felt as though he had reached the apex of his personal journey. He couldn't wrap his mind around the idea, the idea of contentment.

Marisa was overwhelmed by the sensation of having let go. She had, for the moment, chosen herself. She was not a selfish person. She did not know what it was like to put oneself before everyone else. She wondered how she'd move forward. She wanted nothing more than to move towards Harry in every way possible. She did not trust this feeling. Was it happiness? She wondered. This was just a kiss after all. This was nothing more than electrical signals flowing through their bodies, communicating to them all the things they'd thought about but never said. All the glances she had thrown in his direction but never stood around long enough to see if they were returned, were now being communicated to him. But she knew she couldn't be the one to take advantage of this situation. She had to maintain balance. She had to maintain her family's tranquility, and that meant denying herself what she wanted most, Harry. So, she pushed him back.

"Harry," she said as they stood an inch apart. He stared into her eyes. He said nothing, though he heard her. "Harry, this isn't a good idea...we can't do this. I can't. I really..." she stopped herself and took a step away from him. She walked over to the mantle above the fireplace and placed the glass on it.

"Tell me you didn't enjoy kissing me," he said. She rolled her eyes.

"It was the worst kiss ever," she said. He laughed.

"You can't keep pretending you don't have feelings for me Marisa. That's no way to live life, constantly running away from yourself,"

"I'm not running away from myself Harry. I'm choosing to do what's best for my family," she said.

"I don't have your sort of resolve," he said as he walked toward her.

"You could have fooled me," she said as he got closer. This time he did not kiss her. He did not dare try that again. He knew she'd resist him. She would not want to relive those feelings again.

Harry could read her discomfort. It was not the type of discomfort a woman showed when she was around a man, she was afraid of or found distasteful. Marisa's discomfort was the sort a woman showed when she knew she wanted to do the one thing her brain told her she shouldn't do. Marisa had to resist falling more in love with him. But more importantly she had to resist letting him know in any definitive way that she was in love with him. As he stood in front of her, she feared he could read her thoughts. She was no longer as guarded as she was when she first entered his house.

Harry surprised her by wrapping his arms around her, giving her a warm hug as if she had been wrapped by the best blanket money could buy. Marisa sighed, the relief of not being pressured to face herself washing over her body. She sank into his body like lovers are keen to do after lovemaking.

The pain in his body seemed to have disappeared. At least his brain was no longer registering the pain. And so, he hugged her tightly and breathed in her peppermint tinged perfume as she lay her head against his chest.

"How you feel matters," he finally said, "and I'm not saying this just because I want to profit from you being true to yourself," he added. She chuckled.

"Now you're my guru Harry," she said, the sarcasm harkening back to their youth.

Harry held onto her as though letting her go would be detrimental to their respective sanities. He could have stayed in that position for a long time. He wanted nothing more than to stay like that, holding one another, their bodies becoming more and more dependent on each other. He looked down at her as he towered over her, but she would not look up. The resistance was there. Even amidst their communal exchange of air, she resisted being enveloped. Her guard was still up. It was clear to Harry she still did not trust him. She did not trust that he wouldn't hurt her.

After a few minutes, she pulled back from him again. She shook her hands as if shaking off some sort of dizzying spell that had subdued her logical mind. She walked to the mantle and stared into the empty fireplace and then turned to look back at him. Harry had walked into the kitchen and was coming back with a plate and a single blueberry muffin on it, with a sliver of butter on the side along with a thin butter knife.

"Everyone likes blueberry muffins," he said with a happy smile. She shook her head.

"Not people who are allergic to blueberries," she said. He laughed.

"People are allergic to blueberries?" he asked in disbelief, though she suspected he was being playful. Marisa walked over to him and grabbed the plate from his hands and began buttering the muffin.

"I'm not going to share with you," she said. He feigned shock, leaving his mouth open for a moment.

"I understand...listen Marisa..."

"He really should have hit you in the face. You're far too pretty for a man," she said. He smirked.

"Aww, you think I'm handsome, please tell me more," he responded.

"I won't" she said as she bit the muffin. She proceeded to sit on his coffee table. He thought for a second about reproaching her for sitting on his coffee table but refrained from doing so.

"Marisa, I know that it is hard to imagine that anything I say to you about how I feel is true," he started, but she lifted the knife in his direction.

"Nothing you say is true," she said.

"Marisa...I'm developing strong feelings for you..."

"What are these strong feelings you're speaking of?" she said as she took another bite of the muffin.

"Marisa...You know what I did last night?" he asked.

"Probably lay in bed thinking about how much your ribs hurt and wishing you had hit him back as hard as he hit you," she said. He was annoyed, but she wasn't wrong.

"After that part subsided, I stayed up all night thinking about you. Trying to piece together all the moments where you and I could have connected. And all I remember was that you were Margo's quiet little sister who did whatever she wanted you to do," he said.

"Oh wow, how insightful Harry," she said. He took a deep breath.

"My point is that you have spent your entire life being second to Margo,"

"It's a very comfortable place to be,"

"Don't you want more?" he asked.

"You want me to want you Harry, isn't that the bottom line?" she answered.

"What is so wrong with that?" he asked. She scoffed.

"That's selfish Harry," she said. He approached her.

"I think I'm in love with you Marisa,"

"Think? You're not so sure,"

"I'm still working it out myself, give me a break," he said. She put the plate down on the coffee table. Then she brushed her hair away from her face.

"Harry, you have said the same things to my sister. You can't blame a girl for being doubtful, can you?" she said.

Harry had no retort. She was right. Her skepticism was warranted. He hadn't done much up to this point to show her that his interest was genuine. And Marisa was not the type of woman to simply eat up a man's words as if they were golden nuggets. His history with Margo did not help his cause. Here was an instant where one's porous adulations for another proved to be more harmful than beneficial.

"I know that this makes little sense, but sometimes you have to look past your own reasoning and just feel what you feel," he said.

"That makes zero sense Harry," she said. He knew she was right. He was starting to ramble. Whatever he had assumed he'd be able to do to get her to see that he really was interested in her, he was failing.

Just then, Harry's doorbell rang. He was saved for the moment by a chance occurrence. He wasn't expecting anyone to come to his house. Yet he welcomed the interruption as he was floundering. He proved to be human after all. Though he presented well and had always been able to handle any situations of the heart that might have popped up unintentionally, here he was struggling. He was no different from any other man who struggled to execute their crafted plans of seduction, or at least, of loving.

At the door was a scrawny tall teenager with a case of bad acne. His skin looked as though his pores would open at any time and the puss produced would eviscerate any men and women in its presence. Harry felt bad for the young man as he accepted the edible arrangement he was holding in his hands. He tipped the young man and the delivery boy ran off to his car, elated that he had received the biggest tip of his week.

It was in considering the troubles that a tall skinny young man with acne might face in life that Harry came to the conclusion that he was in fact trying too hard. He realized that certain things in life could not be controlled. He could not control his feelings, nor could he control how Marisa felt about him expressing those feelings. The best he could do was to try and influence her thinking. And ultimately that is all any man can do. They can only present the best they have to offer, and hope the woman they desired, could see the gem within them.

And so, when he returned to the living room, he placed the edible arrangement on the table. Without saying a word to Marisa, he read the note that came with the gift. It was from a client of his who had gotten wind of the fact that he had been injured and was sending him a token of appreciation as well as encouragement for a speedy recovery.

"You're loved," she said when he looked up at her.

"In more ways than one," he said. She chuckled. "Sometimes people have a hard time seeing my capacity for love," he said.

"Are we talking about me?"

"No," he replied. He grabbed a cut-up piece of pineapple and put it in his mouth. He sucked on it for a moment and then began to chew. She laughed.

"You're terribly suggestive Harry, it's distasteful," she said. He giggled.

"I think you're saying much more about your own mind then you are making an observation about me," he said.

"So, calculating,"

"It's one of my many qualities,"

"Vanity is not a virtue Harry," she said as she leaned over and grabbed a strawberry.

"Self-adulation is not vain. It takes a lot of work to view yourself in a positive light. People assume that if you are good looking or are thought to be good looking, life is much easier," he said.

"Oh, it's not?" she asked. He shook his head.

"People don't take you seriously if they find you attractive," he said, "they assume you're just putting on an act. They think you're performing,"

"All of life is a performance Harry. Some people are better at it than others, but we are all performing something, including...love," she said. Now she was the one staring at him. Her eyes fixed on his, did not move even when they reached that critical moment of thirty seconds where most people look elsewhere lest someone sees through their soul.

"Love is scary. So, people tend to do their best to not express it unless they know for a fact that it will be reciprocated." he said. Her eyes look brighter during the day than at night, he thought. It was an obvious observation, but he wasn't in a frame of mind to think clearly. He had been captured, though he was not fully aware of it.

"People...they break promises all the time,"

"I don't make promises," Harry responded. She was moving toward him now. It was as if the coffee table between them no longer existed. She somehow seemed to glide across the floor. He was curious to know how she moved so effortlessly from her side of the living room to him, but he did not want to break eye contact.

"I guess...that's a good thing," she said as they came face to face. He'd have kissed her, but there was no question that she was in charge this time around.

Marisa pressed her lips to his, tasting the juicy pineapple from his soft lips. When he returned her kiss, they both seemed to be lifted onto another plane, lost in the moment, forgetting the fact that she wanted to resist, and he wanted to pursue. There were no roles to be played now. She was a different person from the woman who waltzed into his house earlier.

The eyes have been said to be the doorway into someone's soul. And Harry had gotten better at holding his gaze. Once you figure out that looking away sends the opposite message to your intended audience, you learn to hold steady. Harry had learned that lesson. He held steady, and even while they kissed, he did not move. He wanted her to have the impression that everything and anything that was happening in the moment was her decision. There was to be no pressure from him. Even if she pulled back, he would not express disappointment. And she didn't pull back. Marisa kissed him as though he was her possession who had been returned to her after a decade's absence. What she felt in that moment, was akin to love.

CHAPTER TEN
Hearts Win

In all his years living in London, Harry did not depend on an alarm to wake him up in the morning. Yet since his return to Oakwood, he had become more and more dependent on an alarm waking him up while he worked on building his business in his hometown. And as the alarm went off at six in the morning, there was something different about Harry. At least there was something different about the way he bounced out of bed as if he had a purpose in life. It was a sudden emergence, one that even surprised the well-mannered businessman himself.

His sudden raison d'etre had nothing to do with the successful business he was trying to expand into Oakwood. He had had a dream that gave him some insight. Harry had dreamt about death. It was the type of dream that was so lucid that one would believe he or she were actually dead or dying. While most people would fear the unknown meanings behind their dreams, Harry did not. He knew that everything in life was a matter of perspective. He knew that the dream meant that he had to stop overthinking and start taking action.

As he stood in his bathroom shaving his face, he thought about the finality of his human experience. He thought about what he wanted out of the time he had. He could not know with any certainty if he would be afforded more time than anyone else, or if he would be afforded any time at all. Then he began to think about the Hannigan sisters. He thought about Marisa and their growing love for one another. It was the first time he truly allowed himself to think that she too might be in love with him. This made him happy. His wide smile as he shaved was telling. Then he thought about Margo.

Harry's love for Margo was an everlasting one. But it was a love that changed over time. There was an unquestionable infatuation that sustained their interactions with one another. And over time he had come to care about her more than he'd wanted or would be caught admitting. However, it was love at a distance. It was love that could not be materialized. It was love that had become platonic, despite the fact that they were physically intimate. Accepting that this change had taken place was one of the most important aspects of Harry's growth.

He decided then, that part of his expression of love for Margo would be to help her, though she may not want it. And part of his growth would be to express himself in a clear manner regarding his feelings for Marisa, despite the fact that it would likely end up hurting Margo in the process. The phone went off again. He had forgotten to turn the alarm off. It was the distraction he needed to get out of his own head and get ready for the day.

Across town, Margo was nearly packed when the doorbell rang. Emily and Charlotte had just finished their breakfast and were sitting in the living room watching Tom and Jerry. It was Marius who had gotten the girls hooked on the devilish cat and mouse and their games of torment, much to Margo's annoyance. Now in his absence, she did not mind them watching it. It was a way to sneak in their father's influence without having him actually be present.

"Charlotte, honey can you check the system and see who's at the door?" Margo called down and she placed the last bits of clothes in her small suitcase. She waited for a few moments to see if she could hear footsteps. She didn't hear anything because the girls had put the volume on the television high. And as she exited the bedroom, she heard her daughter's sigh.

"It's aunt Marisa Mom!" Charlotte shouted. The little girl opened the door to Marisa and jumped into her arms.

"Hi sweetie, how are you?" Marisa asked and kissed her niece on the cheek. Marisa had a small blue suitcase beside her. She dragged it in behind Charlotte and closed the door.

Margo carried her suitcase down the stairs, somewhat excited to go on a trip with her sister, but all aware of the trepidation that came with the decision to leave her husband exactly where he was. At this point, it was no longer that she did not care what happened to Marius. She did care. But she was punishing him. She was punishing him for daring to put a wrench in her affair with Harry. She was punishing him, for loving her, and allowing that love to lead him to do something careless that could have ruined the lives of everyone involved, including their young daughters.

"Is mom here yet?" Marisa asked as she played with her black headband. Margo tossed her suitcase in the foyer, paying little attention to the fact that it was her belongings in there.

"No, her car broke down so she's taking a car service, she should be here soon...You want something to eat? Drink?" Margo asked.

"I'll take seltzer if you have some," Marisa answered. She followed after her sister into the kitchen.

"Thanks for coming with sis. I really need this escape. I feel like my life is falling apart," Margo said as she handed Marisa the glass of water.

"That's because it is falling apart," Marisa responded.

"I mean you're not supposed to agree Marisa, God,"

"I'm sorry, but you and I have a no lie pact, don't we?" Marisa responded. Margo pondered her response for a few minutes.

"We do, don't we?" Margo asked, Marisa nodded, "And we're supposed to tell each other the truth, no matter what right?"

"Yes, of course, you know that," Marisa said.

"So, what's going on with you and Harry?" Margo asked.

It was a question Marisa dreaded. She could not be surprised by the question. It was something she saw coming. Margo had to have known that there was a sort of tension between Marisa and Harry. It was the type of tension that if built up enough, would result in an outpouring of emotions. Both sisters were filled with dread. Margo feared she'd lost Harry forever, to her sister. And she could not be upset with her sister, as she herself understood that Harry had a capacity to make Marisa happy. Marisa feared that should she confront her feelings about Harry, she would end up hurting her sister.

"There's..."

"The truth Marisa, the actual truth," Margo said. Marisa sighed.

"God, Margo, I've been in love with him for a long time. I'm...I'm sorry, it's not something that I can control. And I haven't done anything with him. I've kept my distance. I wouldn't do anything to hurt you." Marisa finally said. She was in tears by the time she finished her sentence. "I've told him nothing can come of this. I can't bear the thought of making you upset Margo," she added. Margo came over to her sister and hugged her.

"I know Marisa. I know...And... I want you to be happy too. You're my sister and I love you and I don't want to be the reason why you can't find happiness," Margo responded.

Standing behind the two women, was Charlotte who had been watching as her mother and her aunt, both with tears in their eyes, hugged one another. The little girl patiently waited for a moment to say something as neither adult seemed to know that she was there. She cleared her throat after waiting another minute. This caught their attention and they let go of one another.

"Not to break the crying party, but grandma just pulled up," Charlotte said. Margo smiled and wiped her eyes.

"You little rascal," Marisa said as she chased after Charlotte who ran away from her aunt, laughing and skipping.

"Please be careful," Margo shouted as they ran away from her.

A little later, Harry had pulled into the parking lot of the police station and was finishing a draft of a proposal for a client in his car when he finally looked at the time. He had been calling Marisa, but she was not returning his calls. He had decided to heed her plea to help Margo by dropping charges against Marius. While he would have been within his rights to stand his ground and refuse to be of help to the hapless husband of his lover, Harry knew that part of showing Marisa that he was a serious man and was willing to do the work necessary to show her he was genuine, included listening to her.

The officer processing his request, did not look so happy as Harry, in a dark blue suit sat across from her. He wanted to drop charges against Marius and pay the bail to get him out of jail. He couldn't understand why the woman sitting across from him had a disgruntled look on her face. He reasoned that this was her natural disposition and had nothing at all to do with him and why he was there in the first place.

"Are you sure you want to do this?" the officer asked, looking up, her spectacles sliding down her nose.

"Yes, I'm sure," Harry replied.

"He assaulted you," the officer said as she typed on her keyboard, loudly hacking away as though she was going to beat the keyboard into submission.

"Yes, I know. I was present,"

"Don't get smart with me Mr. Melville...I just want to be sure that you know what you're doing. You're dropping charges against the man who assaulted you and you're paying his bail," she said, "is that correct Mr. Melville?"

"Yes, that's correct," Harry responded.

The officer walked away from the desk and disappeared for a few minutes. She returned with a set of papers in her hands. She placed the papers in front of Harry and gave him a pen. Harry handed her his card and she walked away again. And when she was done, she stared at him for a few minutes, as if studying him for signs of mental illness such was her incredulity. Then she told him to return to the lobby and she would get someone to retrieve Marius.

When he stepped out, Marius looked as though he had shed a few pounds. He certainly did not smell like alcohol which was his norm. He looked a bit confused when he realized it was Harry, the man he had assaulted, who was the one who came to get him out. The two men looked at each other, sizing each other up as though what is said next would be a defining moment in both of their lives.

"Uh...I didn't see this coming," Marius said as they walked out of the police station.

"Me neither," Harry replied. They walked over to a bench across the street from the station.

"Look...I'm sorry I did that to you. I never thought...that's not me, usually. That's not how I behave," Marius said as they sat. Harry nodded.

"I understand. And to be fair, I also owe you an apology," Harry responded.

"No...no, you don't owe me anything. In fact, I'm quite shocked that you came here and dropped the charges. I don't know how to thank you," Marius said.

"Look, I knew Margo was married. I never should have baited her, and I should have been more considerate, I wouldn't want anyone doing that to me." Harry said. Marius took a deep breath.

"Thank you. That means a lot," Marius replied.

"Let me drive you home, I think you two have a lot to work through, and I promise I'm going to stay out of your way," Harry said. Marius patted him on the back and nodded.

"I had you pegged wrong," Marius said, "I hope you can forgive me for what happened. My emotions got the best of me," Marius said.

They said little during the ride to Marius and Margo's house. Nothing more needed to be said. The two of them were not friends, and neither one was under the illusion that they were going to develop a friendship after all that happened. At the very least, they were going to tolerate one another. Neither men could configure in his mind, how Margo would react to seeing her husband and her lover together, having moved on from the incident that derailed them all. For his part, Harry hoped that delivering Marius to his home, his family, would force Margo to truly think about what she wants and how she had gone about getting it. He also hoped, though he was beset with doubt, that his gesture of empathy, would awaken Marisa.

However, when they arrived at the house, Marisa and Margo were not there. Their mother was with the kids, surprised to find out that Harry had dropped the charges against her son-in-law. She told both men that the sisters were on their way to the Oakwood airport for their trip to Aruba. The children were overjoyed to see their father, never truly aware of what happened between he and Harry. Aware of the fact that he was essentially a stranger to everyone in his presence, Harry said his goodbyes and left the house, heading straight to the airport.

He hadn't felt this sort angst before in his life. Harry was mentally strong and unwavering. He had always been that way. He succeeded in business because he knew how to keep everything together. He knew how to make the right moves. But now there was no telling what the right moves were. It was, for the first time in his life, a moment to follow his heart. Before this, he couldn't be sure that his heart, his feelings could be trusted. And yet now he had been changed.

As he paced across the floors of the airport towards the ticketing area, his heart started to beat faster as if it was being controlled by a maestro with a firm grasp of his baton. And the closer he got to the designated area, the more he could hear his own heartbeat, louder and louder. His body was increasingly awakened. He was certain the people in the airport would have to call an ambulance to aid him. His body was on fire. He wished he hadn't worn a suit. The heat was too much. He looked around, no one else seemed to be bothered by the airport temperature. He didn't remember airports being this hot. In fact, he remembered that one of the things he hated about airports was the fact that they were always cold. He'd always have to bring a sweater of some kind with him whenever he was traveling.

Marisa noticed him first. It was serendipity. He couldn't have designed the scenario better himself. Their eyes met and for a brief moment, a moment few people would notice, and he himself could have missed, she smiled. There was a lightness in her eyes. It was what masked joy looked like. Because a second later, the smile disappeared as she looked back at her sister. Harry had forgotten for a minute that Margo was there. This was the tale of an interrupted love, one constantly fighting for survival.

"Harry! Wait, what are you doing here?" Margo said when she saw him. Of course, she would be the first to speak, he thought. Margo never saw a room she couldn't dominate. Given time, he imagined, she would dominate the airport with her energy. "You look, hot," she added. Harry wiped his forehead with the back of his hand.

"Your mom said you two were headed here," he said, breathing heavily.

"Do you want some water?" Marisa asked. He shook his head. The sisters, he thought, were very good at playing to type. Marisa, more caring than Margo, but unable to take advantage of any situation where she would come out the victor.

"I'm okay," he said as he finally was able to stand up straight. He turned his face to Marisa, as if Margo was not present. "I dropped the charges against Marius and bailed him out. That's why I was at the house," he said to Marisa. She smiled. That light came back again. She approved.

"Why on earth would you do such a thing Harry?" Margo asked.

"Because I understand. I understand everything. I've never had to work hard for anything in my life. Most things have been easy. But now, I get it. I understand that sometimes you have to show yourself to prove to someone that you're the real deal. So, I'm showing myself," he said.

"Harry, I really wish you hadn't done that," Margo said as she pulled him back to look him in the face.

"Margo, there is a man at your house who loves you more than anything in the world,"

"I don't owe him anything, he is not the man I married," she said.

"You're right. You don't owe him anything. And yes, he has made some really stupid mistakes. He may even have taken you for granted. But he loves you. And I think after everything, he is more than ready to face up to his mistakes," Harry said.

"I really just cannot understand why you are standing up for him after everything that he has done to you Harry," she said, dropping her suitcase to the ground. Harry turned to Marisa.

"Because sometimes love makes people do the craziest things," he said. The smile showed up again. "Marisa, I'm in love with you. I know it is hard for you to understand that given everything that has happened. And I know you've told me why it can't be true, but for the first time in my life, I really feel something in my heart. And it's not lust for your body alone...it's...it's deeper, and it gets me excited and awakened," he added. Margo had a look of horror on her face as though she had been delivered the worst news of her life.

"Harry," Margo said.

"Harry," Marisa said

Marisa barely had enough time to fully formulate her sentence when Harry, who had been a foot away from her, pulled her closer to him. He kissed her as though it was the last time, they were going to see one another. He held onto her as their lips became electrified by the magic of love. And though she hadn't wanted to let go, she could not help herself. She kissed him back, sensually pulling on his lips as though drawing the delectable juices from a forbidden fruit. Then she quickly pulled back away from him.

"Margo...oh Margo, I'm so sorry. I'm so sorry...I shouldn't have...I'm sorry," Marisa said. Margo started laughing. She laughed so hard that it drew the attention of people nearby. Harry was confused, and Marisa afraid of what her sister would do next.

"It's...honey, you don't have to apologize to me. I don't own him dear. Harry is his own man. And... he's never told me he loved me," Margo said much to their surprise. "Marisa, I love you...and you deserve to be in love. And you deserve to be with someone who loves you. So... I'm going to be okay. I'm going to be fine. And you and I... we're going to be fine. We are sisters. We are bonded for life," she added.

"I just..." Marisa started, and Margo hugged her.

"I'm going to transfer my ticket to Harry," Margo said.

"Margo, you don't have to do that. I don't want to interrupt your trip," Harry said. Margo laughed.

"Too late for that...but Harry, if you hurt my sister...even the slightest, you will regret it," Margo said as she hugged him.

"Thank you, Margo," Marisa said.

Margo knew she was doing the right thing, despite the fact that she was heartbroken. She did not want her sister to see that she was gutted by the idea of her and Harry being together. But she hadn't lied about loving Marisa. And she knew that Harry was a good person and would treat her sister right. So, as she walked away from them, tears running down her face, she thought about what lay ahead of her. She was certain, despite what Harry said about Marius, that she did not want to remain married to him. She loved the idea of a man loving her so much that he would do something irrational. What she couldn't shake was the fact that he came so close to taking someone else's life. That to her, was not a show of love. It was an expression of uncontrollable rage. She did not want to stick around to see that come up again.

Harry and Marisa stood in place for a while, both surprised by the ease with which Margo handled the situation. They flitted between moments of deep sighs and staring at one another, and moments of deep kisses and embraces that suggested they were long lost lovers. Harry felt peace in his chest, as if a weight had been lifted. Her smile stayed for a while, and he framed it in his mind.

The End

Thanks for reading!

DID YOU LIKE THIS BOOK?

I NEED YOU...
Without reviews, indie books are impossible to market. Leaving a review will only take a minute. It doesn't need to be long, just a sentence or two telling people what you liked about the book. This will give others an idea of why they might like it too. It will also help me in writing more stories about these characters.
Few Rockstar readers leave reviews, and it would mean the world to me if you could be one of those.

Thank You!
TARA C. GODDARD

Don't miss out!

Click the button below and you can sign up to receive emails whenever Tara C. Goddard publishes a new book. There's no charge and no obligation.

1

https://books2read.com/r/B-A-TWRJ-CZCDB

BOOKS 2 READ

Connecting independent readers to independent writers.

Also by Tara C. Goddard

Oakwood
Dorian and Julia: Oakwood Book One[2]
The Hannigan Sisters: Oakwood Book Two[3]
Blue Falls[4]
The Rose Proposal[5]

Watch for more at Tara C. Goddard's site[6].

---

2. https://www.draft2digital.com/catalog/511173

3. https://www.draft2digital.com/catalog/511708

4. https://www.draft2digital.com/catalog/531831

5. https://www.draft2digital.com/catalog/564888

6. http://www.tcgoddard.com